Lady Delilah Dares A Duke

Windermeres in Love Series
Book Four

Sofie Darling

ARE YOU SIGNED UP FOR DRAGONBLADE'S BLOG?

You'll get the latest news and information on exclusive giveaways, exclusive excerpts, coming releases, sales, free books, cover reveals and more.

Check out our complete list of authors, too!

No spam, no junk. That's a promise!

Sign Up Here

www.dragonbladepublishing.com

Dearest Reader;

Thank you for your support of a small press. At Dragonblade Publishing, we strive to bring you the highest quality Historical Romance from some of the best authors in the business. Without your support, there is no 'us', so we sincerely hope you adore these stories and find some new favorite authors along the way.

Happy Reading!

CEO, Dragonblade Publishing

Additional Dragonblade books by Author Sofie Darling

Windermeres in Love Series
Mr. Sinclair Beguiles a Bluestocking (Prequel)
Lady Amelia Takes a Lover (Book 1)
Lord Archer Catches a Contessa (Book 2)
Miss Windermere Woos a Highlander (Book 3)
Lady Delilah Dares a Duke (Book 4)

Dedication

To Eric, my forever love

Prologue

Eton College, England
Summer 1819

THE FIRST FEW steps Delilah took onto the stage stuttered with hesitation. A surprise, that. After all, this moment was all she'd ever wanted.

Then one step gained momentum after another and she was standing in the center, lights bright upon her, awareness of the audience's rapt attention skittering across her skin, fizzing through every last nerve ending.

Alive.

That was how she felt in this moment.

Utterly and entirely alive with a joy she'd never before experienced.

She was here, upon a real stage, acting in front of a real audience.

She opened her mouth to speak her first line.

"Lady Delilah?" rang out into the silence.

Delilah blinked and immediately shook off the notion that the question had been intended for her. There could be any number of Lady Delilah's in the audience.

Ignoring it, she opened her mouth again.

"Why," came the voice again—louder, clearer…*certain.*

Delilah's ear picked up a note in that voice, too. *Familiar.*

"I do believe it truly is Lady Delilah Windermere."

All eyes widened on her—and something happened within those eyes. They saw *her*—Lady Delilah Windermere. A lady who had no business being on this stage or anywhere near it.

In an instant, three available options came to her.

She could collapse to the stage boards in tears, a sniveling cowardly mess.

She could laugh it off and say the joke was on them.

She could sink to her knees in shame and offer her most abject apologies.

So many options...

None of them tolerable.

Instead, she squared up to the audience, who were growing unsettled in their seats and louder in their murmurings, and pulled herself up to her full five-foot, ten-inch height before lowering into a deep curtsey. When she rose, she wore the broadest—and falsest—smile of her life. She even received a thin, uncertain scattering of applause.

But she didn't budge from her patch of stage. Instead, she stood there, immovable, silent, her eyes slowly, carefully raking across the crowd until...

They landed on the owner of that voice—a voice she'd known since her brother Archie had brought him home on school break years ago—with his tousled dark blond hair and golden eyes that held the power to mesmerize. Not her, of course, but she'd overheard more than a few young ladies rhapsodize about those eyes.

His Grace Sebastian Crewe, the Duke of Ravensworth.

His usual air of sardonic gravity hung about him like a dense cloak, vibrating with the energy specific to him. For a mad moment, she entertained the possibility that Archie had sent this duke to cheat her out of her triumph—for it was clear she'd been on the verge of winning their bet. He'd posited she couldn't make it through the short summer term at Eton as a boy. Delilah had posited that she could. A bet had been made.

She shook off the idea. Archie was a lot of things, but he was no cheat. No, this was all Ravensworth with his cool, assessing gaze that didn't flinch or shift away from her unrelenting glare.

Delilah had never had an enemy—not before this moment.

And now she had one for life.

He'd had a choice.

He could've kept quiet and allowed her this moment.

Instead, he'd swept in and ruined everything—and for no better reason than to amuse a crowd or...

Himself.

In truth, his motivation didn't matter. He'd tried to humiliate her and destroy her dream. While he'd succeeded in the latter, he wouldn't in the former. It was up to her to scramble out from under this mess.

"Blow, winds, crack your cheeks! Rage! Blow!" her voice rang out, quieting the increasingly restive crowd with her favorite speech from *King Lear*. As Shakespeare's words flowed from her mouth, the entrancement specific to live performance took over the theater. For these precious few seconds, the audience saw not Lady Delilah Windermere, but a half-mad, wandering king. Yet her gaze remained steadily fixed on one man as she spoke the words, *"You owe me no subscription. Then let fall your horrible pleasure."*

Ravensworth didn't shrink from her scorn. Instead, his usual sardonic smile curled about his mouth.

"O! O! 'tis foul!" she finished on a howl and collapsed onto the stage.

Dead silence filled the theater, the audience transfixed...

By *her.*

She pushed herself to a stand and curtseyed for the second time tonight.

Off stage left, the headmaster recovered his surely overwhelmed nerves—*a lady at Eton College!*—and made straight for her, sputtering with great indignation. *"You...you...you!"* was all he could get out.

Delilah decided it best she hitch her robes to her knees, exit

3

stage right, and leg it—all the way back to London.

Her time at Eton College was quite finished.

As she streaked across the campus dusky with encroaching night, taking the snickets and alleyways used mostly by servants and delinquent students—the latter of which described her, at the moment—unreleased emotion formed a tight knot in the center of her chest. So, this was what heartbreak felt like. The feeling that she'd had all she ever wanted sitting in the palm of her hand, only to have it snatched away.

Once she reached her rooms, she didn't bother changing out of her costume as she collected the coin pouch she'd stuffed into her mattress for this exact emergency. She left her other belongings behind—after all, they belonged to a boy who didn't actually exist—and again raced through the snickets and alleyways that would avoid the night watch as she made her way off the grounds and down the road.

She passed one, then another, coaching inn. They were simply too close, and Ravensworth might be in pursuit.

So he could gloat.

Which simply could not be borne.

The muted, relentless *thud-thud-thud* of approaching horse hooves sounded behind her, growing louder. Instinctively, she sidestepped off the road and sank down into a boggy ditch that had her feet soaked in cold mud up to her ankles. She folded herself into a tight crouch and soaked her bottom, too.

What a night.

She counted rapid heart and hoof beats until horse and rider galloped past.

Ravensworth.

She knew it with a certainty absolute and sickening. He wasn't the sort of man to let pass an opportunity to bask in his superiority.

Well, that bloody superior man wouldn't be finding her tonight.

Pent-up tears sprang forward, blurring her vision. All sorts of tears—tears of sadness…tears of frustration…tears of anger.

It was that last emotion she would hang onto once the others had worn themselves out.

But she wouldn't shed those tears—not yet.

Not until she reached the safety of her bedroom at Casa Windermere and turned the lock behind her.

Then enough tears to fill the Thames would burst the dam and flow.

And there was but one man to blame for tonight's triumph turned to ashes.

Ravensworth.

She wouldn't soon forget.

Chapter One

Lincolnshire, England
August 1822

S EBASTIAN SPOTTED HIS quarry across the spacious ballroom
and began to move.

Tonight was the final night of the house party he'd been
throwing in the wilds of Lincolnshire, which meant a ballroom
flowing with champagne and laughter, packed with aristocratic
and local bodies alike swathed in superfine, silk, and diamonds—
bodies sheened in the perspiration specific to a lively late-summer
gathering.

Navigating the room, all eight chandeliers lit to rival the
heavens, Sebastian's usual opaque smile remained firmly affixed
to his mouth as he kept the lord who had been pointedly avoiding
him all night in his sights. This smile of Sebastian's happened to
be his mouth's natural resting place. It also happened to be a
smile that was expected of him. The *ton* would be sorely
disappointed if the Duke of Ravensworth suddenly threw a jolly
laugh up to the chandeliers and sprayed joy all over the gathering.

He was the Duke.

And he was more than that.

He was the very image of a duke that people formed in their
minds when they thought of a duke—serious-minded...not easily
amused...not an ounce of frivolity on him. Which wasn't to say
he was a dour, humorless piece of work, but the world he

inhabited had taught him one very important lesson.

Everyone wanted something from a duke—his attention…his approval…his smile.

But here was what he knew.

He didn't have to give them any of it.

Although what the man he sought—*Viscount Wakeley*—wanted from him was to be left alone.

A chuckle escaped Sebastian, which the lady he happened to be slipping past at the moment—the newly wed Countess of Bridgewater, who had promised £200 for the new arts building in London this house party was in the service of funding—must've thought was for her given the saucy flash of the eye she tossed him over her shoulder.

Sebastian kept moving. That particular lady's husband was known to have been deeply possessive of his mistresses. Sebastian assumed a wife would be no different. Nothing he wanted to get tangled up with, anyway.

Most—lords and ladies alike—vied for his attention, albeit usually for differing reasons. The lords were generally easier to manage than their ladies, who viewed the imminently eligible Duke of Ravensworth's unattached status as invitation or challenge for conquest. In general, he'd learned early to steer clear of such entanglements, leaving him with a reputation more salacious than his lived reality.

The fact was he wasn't a licentious or idle duke. Instead, he maintained tight control of every aspect of his life, as many depended and relied upon him. Yet over the years, the image and truth of the Duke of Ravensworth had become so intertwined, he wasn't sure if at this point in his three and thirty years even he would be able to separate them—if he felt the urge.

Which he didn't, for the record.

Ahead, Wakeley made a mistake. He allowed his wife to pull him into conversation with a large group. Sebastian saw his opportunity and seized it, efficiently cutting across gleaming mahogany and only stopping once he reached the periphery of the loose circle, which parted in an instant to allow him a place.

In truth, he appreciated the way people responded to his presence. Expectations were set and clear. All who attended a soirée, house party, or ball thrown by the Duke of Ravensworth knew why they'd been invited, and if they accepted the invitation—which, of course, they would—they'd end the evening lighter in the pockets.

Such was the price to attend this duke's gatherings, for Sebastian didn't invite just anyone. Meticulous curation went into his lists. Some nobles he invited because of their freedom with their purses—whether by true wealth or credit wasn't his concern. Others were motivated by appearances—to be seen at a duke's ball. He was more than happy to emblazon their names on a building for a generous donation.

"Ravensworth," said one lord in greeting. *Mossdown*. He'd pledged £500 a few months ago.

Sebastian gave a nod. "I must offer my appreciation for your generous promise of a donation last spring."

"'Twas nothing, Your Grace," said Mossdown, a crimson blush creeping above his cravat.

Appreciation from a duke… It was a coveted thing.

Yet another power Sebastian was able to wield.

"True," he said, nodding, "your promise was nothing." A few lords shifted uncomfortably on their feet, and a few ladies tittered nervously behind their fans. "But your fulfillment of the promise was much appreciated." Even as tension released from the group, Sebastian caught Wakeley's dodgy eye. "If only everyone delivered on their promises."

The sum Wakeley owed was a mere hundred pounds. But that was beside the point. He must pay. What was the point of an honor system without honor? Society would crumble on its ear.

Wakeley swallowed.

"Some don't?" asked one lady with surprised lift of an eyebrow.

"You'd be shocked," said Sebastian, refusing to release Wakeley's gaze.

"But it's for the arts," said another lady.

"Does anyone have suggestions for collection?" asked Sebastian, lightly. Conversations about money weren't the done thing in his circles, but here they were and he had a point to make to one specific lord. "I can't very well send a burly Runner out for collection."

This got a laugh from all. Wakeley swallowed, again.

"Oh, I think a public shaming would do nicely," said yet another lady.

"Interesting," said Sebastian with a cock of his head. "Do go on."

What was truly interesting was that it was Wakeley's wife making the case for a public shaming.

Her face lit with an idea. "You could call him on it at a party."

"A party such as this one?" asked Sebastian.

Wakeley turned an unhealthy shade of chartreuse.

"Exactly," said the man's wife without the faintest notion of her husband's suffering at her side.

Sebastian bowed to Lady Wakeley before shifting his gaze toward her husband. "A suggestion I'll take under advisement for my next party."

Wakeley wiped his sweaty brow with the back of his hand and released a long, slow breath. He seemed to have gotten the message that Sebastian wouldn't be exposing him tonight. But he wouldn't be so lucky in the future.

Sebastian had a feeling he would be receiving the £100 within the week.

Of course, he could endow a new arts building in London from foundation to roof and everything in between without blinking an eye, but that was beside the point. It was vital that the *ton* threw their money at it, too. With financial investment came emotional investment, and as a duke of considerable wealth and influence, Sebastian was just the duke to shame the *ton* into financing their entertainments.

If they wanted the pleasure of the arts, they must invest in them. He saw this as his duty, obligation, and life's work.

And if he sometimes grew weary of all the duty and obligation he'd carried with him since the moment of his birth—his father had perished in a boating accident a month before he was born—he kept it to himself. For he understood his place of entitlement. The price for the privileged life he led was small.

The simple fact was he'd shouldered responsibility from the day he was born, and he didn't mind those responsibilities. He was good at being a duke—he *liked* being a duke.

But after Cambridge, he'd taken a long look at his life and the lives of the aristocratic men around him and noticed something. His interest in the arts afforded him a view of life beyond his title. A life that provided spaces where he could flirt with freedom and taste a life altogether different from his. The sort of life he could never immerse himself fully within, but those with the talent, will, and drive could. Each partnership was as unique as each artist. An opera singer would have a different set of goals from a sculptor or a composer from a poet.

"Now, if you'll excuse me," he said on a shallow bow, "I must ensure the champagne flows until dawn."

He knew it would, of course, but he'd found that particular excuse to be the most effective. The champagne must flow in an endless stream. And the crapulence and aching heads on the morrow... Well, that was better left to tomorrow.

His mission complete, he pointed his feet in the direction of his study, where he kept a careful log of all the promised—and fulfilled—donations. He had a few to jot down from tonight, and he couldn't very well have his private secretary following him around at parties and transcribing every pledge. That would spoil the illusion a bit.

"Ah, if it isn't His Grace himself," came a broad, brandy-soaked voice that veered a mile wide of aristocratic.

Sebastian schooled his features before turning. "Mr. Shaw, how good of you to attend our little soirée."

Mr. Shaw was a manufacturer of steam engines who was looking to use his recently acquired wealth to gain a foothold in Society and perhaps a title along the way, either through service to the Crown—the hard way—or through a daughter's marriage—the more achievable way. There was always a down-on-his-luck young buck looking to recover the family's fortunes through a marriage to an heiress.

And Sebastian was more than willing to aid this endeavor for a little *quid pro quo*. For the fact was he didn't give two tosses about titles, though he wouldn't confess as much to a soul in this increasingly sweat-soaked ballroom. These particular souls' primary concern was of title and status. It would be insulting to their view of the world if he scoffed that it was all silly vanity and pretense. So, he also courted men like Shaw—those with first-generation wealth. They were usually the most eager to give to his causes, anyway.

A jolly laugh burst forth from the man as he pointedly glanced about the ballroom that sparkled to the rhythms of string quartet and bursts of laughter. "Quite a *little* party you throw, Ravensworth."

Sebastian enjoyed the company of men such as Shaw. Plain spoken, yet ever with an air of levity. One could relax in the company of such a man. Still, Sebastian suspected a core of steel within Shaw and intuited his business rivals might feel less at ease in his presence.

A canny glint entered Shaw's eye. Sebastian knew that glint. "And all arranged without the assistance of a wife?" asked Shaw.

And there it was.

Sebastian knew he was viewed as a somewhat unusual duke. A bachelor duke. A guest list was usually the purview of a wife, and he didn't have one of those—not even the twinkling of one in his eye.

"Or perhaps there's a duchess on the horizon?" continued Shaw, perhaps emboldened by Sebastian's silence.

The image of a woman—tall and willowy with short blonde

curls and glacial azure eyes that mostly twinkled with mischief, except when they landed on him and shifted to barely suppressed fury—flashed across his mind.

He blinked the image away and dismissed it, as usual.

Though most didn't ask the question with such affable bluntness, it was a question to which Sebastian was accustomed, even when asked in subtler ways. Which made it a question he knew how to evade effectively with a self-effacing smile and shake of the head that told no one anything.

But just as Sebastian had been a man on a mission earlier, so too, was Shaw tonight. He had three daughters of marriageable age—and Sebastian wouldn't be marrying any of them. Which wasn't a conversation he was keen on having with this man tonight—or ever. Still, he could appreciate the ambition, though sorely misplaced.

So, he decided it expedient to speak the language Shaw understood best. The plain sort. "I can expect delivery of your pledge by...?"

Shaw snorted. "My man will have it to you by day's end tomorrow." The man's eyes narrowed. "And I can expect the invitation to your fancy London ball for myself and my family by...?"

A half smile tipped about Sebastian's mouth. Now they were back on solid *quid pro quo* ground. "Day's end tomorrow."

Every year, he held a ball on the equinox to herald the end of summer and the arrival of autumn. This year it was to be held on the twenty-third of September, only six or so weeks from now. It was one of the most exclusive invitations in the *ton*'s social calendar. And since Mr. Shaw had promised £2,000 to the funding of the arts building, the man had acquired for himself and his family one of those exclusive invitations. Sebastian reckoned favorable odds that at least one of the daughters would find herself a titled husband on that night.

The men gave each other a nod of mutual understanding, and Sebastian excused himself. Again, his feet pointed toward his study, but this time they reached their destination.

A few minutes later, Sebastian was inside and twisting the key in the door lock. He'd learned over the years that if he entered an empty room at a soirée alone, someone was always bound to follow—be it a gentleman who saw his opportunity for a private word with a duke or a lady who wanted privacy of a different variety.

Sure enough, the handle rattled.

He released a snort and made straight for the brandy cart. He didn't imbibe spirits when mingling at these soirées. They were a sort of work. As his guests turned a little fuzzy about the edges, he stayed sharp. He often thought he could've been a top-notch swindler had he been born beneath a different moon and circumstances. But he wasn't a fleecer of the aristocracy; simply a determined patron of the arts, which benefited society as a whole.

He took his brandy onto the private terrace that could only be accessed through the study and stared into the garden lit by a hundred flickering, candlelit globes. At last, he allowed a feeling of accomplishment release. He'd secured £3,000 pounds tonight. He counted it as a success for a house party thrown in the wilds of Lincolnshire.

A feminine voice reached him from below. "Jem, tomorrow's the Albion Players' final night. I heard they got a strong man with 'em this year."

Sebastian poked his head over the stone balustrade to find two servants on the lawn. He shifted back far enough so they wouldn't notice him. The servants deserved to enjoy a stroll in an enchanted night garden, too, without a duke spoiling their good time.

"Elsie, ye know I like a strong man," said Jem. "I'll see if Old Sam will take me place in the stables tomorrow night."

Elsie flashed a dimpled smile at Jem, whose shoulders relaxed in an instant. "Meet me at eight in the village square and don't be late," she tossed over her shoulder. "I have to get back to that Mrs. Montague. She spilled wine on her new white silk gown, and

she's in a right flutter about it. Red wine and a white gown..."
Her eyes rolled toward the heavens.

"Nobs," Jem scoffed, dismissive, even as he turned in the opposite direction, presumably returning to his own duties for the night.

Reading between the lines of Jem and Elsie's conversation, Sebastian understood there was a traveling theater company in the area. The village square, to be exact. How long had it been since he'd attended a pantomime?

Years.

He decided in an instant that tomorrow night's show would have an additional audience member. Of course, he wouldn't go as himself, but dressed down. He still had clothes from when he, Archie, and Rory would hit the East End incognito. In certain circumstances, it was better that an aristo didn't flaunt his social status.

A frisson of excitement traced through him. The fact was as much as he enjoyed the high arts, he enjoyed the low variety equally well. Each occupied a rightful place in society. Traveling companies were lively and fun and, truly, when was the last time he'd done something purely for the fun of it? The trip to Italy with Archie and his sisters?

He shook his head. Those wild Windermeres. What adventure weren't they equal to?

The truth was he missed his friends. Amelia and her duke were loved up in London, relentlessly producing one babe after another. Archie and Valentina were presently en route home from the Continent, at last. Rory and Juliet had taken to running a farm in Scotland and spouting poetry at any animal within listening distance. And Delilah... She'd up and bolted to Switzerland, of all places.

They all seemed to have proceeded with the rest of their lives.

Without him.

He gave himself a mental shake. What was this? Was he

turning into a self-pitying noble—the worst sort of noble there was?

Right.

Tomorrow night, he would have a bit of fun—the sort unencumbered by the duties of a duke or feelings of self-piteousness.

Chapter Two

S EBASTIAN STEPPED ONTO the village green and tugged his slouch hat lower over his forehead, hoping his identity wouldn't be obvious to all. He had no desire to foreground himself and make people uncomfortable while they were enjoying their night.

So far, no one had cut him a second glance.

Of course, why would they?

Though the evening had gone gray with approaching night, the green was bright with the atmosphere of a festival. A magician here. An acrobat there. A terrier dressed as Queen Elizabeth dancing for treats on its hind legs, grabbing giggles from children and their parents alike. A stallholder thrusting a sugar plum into his face. "Three fer a ha'penny."

Sebastian dug into a pocket and found a linty shilling.

The stallholder's eyes went wide. "That'll do."

And Sebastian was left holding a bag full of sugar plums.

Sugar plum incident notwithstanding, it felt good to move through the crowd like a ghost. No one deferred to him here—a freedom enjoyed the more for its rarity.

He popped a sweet into his mouth and kept walking. Most villages didn't allow theater companies use of their village green. Usually, they had to ask a local gentleman for use of his land.

Sebastian supposed that was why he hadn't been aware of their presence in the area. The village had granted them the necessary permission.

He experienced a strange stab in his chest. No one would've thought to invite the local duke who only graced them with his presence two or three times a year to throw a country house party.

And he didn't blame them.

He wouldn't invite the local duke either. Dukes were a reliably dour, unimaginative lot.

He snorted.

A small puckish lad scampered across the stage—the terrier Queen Elizabeth prancing behind him—and began lighting the lanterns, one by one, which would not only illuminate the night's entertainments, but also the company's sign in bright crimson and gold—*Ye Olde Albion Players*.

Sebastian took a standing place at the farthest edge of the audience. He'd always appreciated the egalitarian nature of theater. Everyone who watched was entitled to an opinion, and everyone's opinion was equally valid, because it came from a place of the truth that resided solely within them. The same applied to all the arts.

Once the performers took to the stage, Sebastian felt himself entering the spell of the pantomime—a mixture of popular scenes from various plays—the sorts of scenes that pulled a laugh…or drew a tear—broken up by a song here, an acrobat there, a few magic tricks to hold the attention. *Clever*. In a festival atmosphere, spans of attention tended to run short. Ye Olde Albion Players understood their audience wouldn't be in the mood for a three-hour production of *Macbeth*. Instead, the full gamut of emotion would be run across their stage tonight.

He knew a lady who would be thoroughly delighted to be here. The same lady who had flashed across his mind last evening. A lady he'd resolved not to think about.

Ever.

She despised him.

Half an hour into the performance—Sebastian's arms crossed over his chest, shoulder propped against an elm—an actress entered stage left. Not as a main player, but as a member of the chorus. His brow crinkled, as unconsciously he pushed off the elm and straightened, sudden tension entering his body.

Tall...willowy...short blonde curls tucked behind her ears...clear azure eyes that flashed mischief at the crowd...

She reminded him of a lady. Nay, not *a* lady. A specific lady. *Lady Delilah Windermere.*

He blinked and squinted and allowed recognition to steal in.

She *was* Lady Delilah Windermere.

He stood, motionless, his eyes refusing to tear themselves away from her as she strutted, strode, danced, and flounced from one end of the stage to the other, the crowd around him reacting to her antics. It could've simply been her unusual height for a woman or her undeniable beauty, but Delilah held more within her and radiated it outward tenfold—a charisma that made it impossible to move one's eyes from her.

Further, Delilah was possessed of the most wonderfully expressive face. A face that conveyed openness. The sort of face that drew in the audience and made it believe and held it in its grip until the very end of a performance and into the breathless moment just beyond, before everyone broke out into a frenzy of applause. She was, quite simply, transfixing.

And she was the daughter of an earl—a lady who absolutely didn't cavort with low company such as Ye Olde Albion Players for the public's consumption.

He snorted.

Right.

Lady Delilah and all the Windermeres did as they pleased.

And as she didn't appear to be in any imminent danger, he settled back against the elm and allowed the performance to proceed without interruption.

This wasn't at all like Eton.

His interference wasn't necessary tonight.

An hour later, the players took their final bows, and the crowd began to thin, and Sebastian knew he should turn on his heel and leave exactly the way he'd come.

What he shouldn't do was seek out Lady Delilah Windermere. Yet…

His feet had other ideas as they led him along the dark periphery of the crowd and toward the company's caravans circled behind the stage. Scatterings of conversations passed him by as he strode through the makeshift camp, glancing about and even poking his head through a few caravan curtains. "And good riddance to that Jed. He barely knew the business end of a hammer from the other," came a gravelly voice here. "Listen, Mary, if you don't want a pin poke in the bottom, you'll hold still," came another there.

It was the third caravan he peeked into that was the charm.

There, seated alone at a dressing table, sat Delilah rubbing at her face with a cloth, removing black stage make-up from her eyebrows, pink from her cheeks, red from her lips, revealing the delicate, fine-boned face beneath, one swipe at a time. *Exquisite.* It was an undisputed fact that Lady Delilah Windermere stood to be a diamond of the first water—if only she would be.

But a description of Lady Delilah's looks only scratched the surface of her. It so happened that her beauty wasn't the most important—or interesting—thing about her.

It was what lay beneath that delicate, exquisite surface.

Determination…talent…intelligence…passion…desire…

Sebastian only realized he'd been watching her for a few seconds too long when a voice rang out, "Now, what sort of Tom do we have peeping into our caravan?"

Sebastian only now noticed the space held two other occupants—actresses by the saucy look of them in various states of dishabille, one removing her boots, the other already down to chemise and stays. The smiles they flashed his way suggested they didn't mind him here in the least.

It was the third set of lips he remained focused upon—lips turned down in a decided frown when her gaze shifted and her eyes met his in the mirror. Delilah's hand froze mid-swipe. The moment stretched as a symphony of emotions marched across her expressive face—*confusion...disbelief...annoyance...anger.*

"Bloody hell," she exclaimed, twisting around on the stool and meeting his gaze directly. "It's *you.*"

Sebastian didn't flinch at the way she flung that *you* at him.

"*Again.*"

"Well acquainted with one another, are we?"

Delilah's gaze flew to the other two actresses. She'd clearly forgotten their presence. "Flora, Dorie, would you mind allowing us a few moments of privacy?" she asked politely, but firmly.

Flora and Dorie's gaze raked over Sebastian again. "No need to get all hoity-toity about it," said one.

"Oh, come now, Dorie. Can't hardly blame the chit for wanting *a few moments of privacy* with this bloke," said Flora with a waggle of her eyebrows.

Laughter trailed in their wake as they cleared out, brushing their bodies against Sebastian's as they did so. Silence prevailed inside the caravan while he and Delilah continued to stare at one another.

Eton.

That was the history that hung between them now that they found themselves alone. He didn't blame her for heaping scorn and anger upon his head. From her perspective, he deserved it. So be it. For here was the thing: even if he could, he wouldn't go back three years and change his actions that night.

He'd kept her safe.

Even if she didn't know it.

And here was the other thing: he didn't want her to know. For that knowledge might influence her to change the way she navigated the world.

And he didn't want her to be ruled by fear.

He wanted a world where Lady Delilah Windermere could

be wild and free.

"Are you determined to ruin every last good thing that I do for myself?" she asked with simmering fury.

"I'll answer that question after you've answered one for me," he said equably.

Her eyes the blue of the Arctic Sea went narrow and wary. "What is it?"

"What are *you* doing *here*?"

Her mouth snapped shut.

It was a rare thing to silence a Windermere, but he could take no joy from it, for he wanted the answer.

An actress in a traveling theater company... What in the blazes was Lady Delilah Windermere playing at?

RAVENSWORTH...

Here.

Delilah's brow furrowed until it hurt, and she gave her head a shake, as if he were a figment of the imagination that could be easily dispelled.

But, no, there he stood, all six feet, two or three inches of solid duke crouched in the low, narrow doorway of the caravan that she shared with Flora and Dorie, implacable.

This man with his dirty blond hair poking from beneath a slouch hat and eyes the gold of an evening sunset on a field of wheat was handsome in the devastating way that made the breath catch in ladies' chests and set fans fluttering in his wake was no concern of Delilah's. He never had been. For while she could observe his handsomeness, she'd never been compelled to consider it directly.

It was that superior attitude of his—like he knew what was good for people better than they knew for themselves.

Quite simply, he was *very* much a duke.

And Delilah had no use for dukes. She knew her mind. She

knew what she wanted. And yet...

How was it that every time she pursued her wants and desires this...*duke!*...arrived to plant himself in the way? First, Eton, and now Ye Olde Albion Players.

Truly, she'd just experienced the best two months of her life.

A wave of anger surged. Well, she simply wouldn't allow Ravensworth to muck this up for her. She was a full-fledged woman of four and twenty years who was capable of forging her own path.

And this duke would know it.

But first... "You know Flora and Dorie think we..." Delilah felt a hot blush rise to the rhythm of her racing heart. It was simply a sentence she couldn't finish.

"Aye," he said, utterly unbothered.

That bit of business out of the way, the pressing question flew from her mouth. "Ravensworth, what are you doing here?" She wasn't about to allow him to backfoot her.

He shrugged. "Enjoying a night's entertainment."

Only now was she able to take in his attire. "And what are you doing dressed like that?" She swept her arm up and down to indicate his entire person from slouch hat to plain workman's clothes to dusty brown boots.

"Dressed like what?" he asked. As if he didn't know.

"Like a...a...a *man.*"

He shifted his shoulder against the doorframe and crossed his arms over his chest. A blaze of something flashed behind his eyes. "Oh, I can assure you," he said, usual sardonic smile coming to a curl about his mouth. "I am very much a man."

Now that her body had begun heating up, it couldn't seem to stop. Beads of sweat would be dripping down her face before long. But he couldn't possibly know that—*could he?*—so she pressed on. "You know exactly what I mean. Why aren't you dressed as your usual dukely self?" Before he could answer, she held up a staying hand. "Wait, what are you doing here at all?" A suspicion flared, and her eyes narrowed. "Are you following me?"

Another suspicion reared its head. "Did Archie—or worse, *Amelia*—send you?"

Ravensworth snorted and shook his head. "I so happened to be at one of my country estates when I heard of the traveling theater company in the area."

Now it was Delilah's turn to snort. "Is there any county in England where you don't own property?"

He didn't miss a beat. "Cornwall."

The flickering light from the caravan's single lantern caught the line of his jaw, illuminating its strong line and day's growth of golden stubble. She couldn't help wondering if he knew of the effect it had on her. *Most definitely.* She'd never met a man more supremely aware of his effect on the world.

He cocked his head. "Aren't you supposed to be spending the summer in Switzerland?"

Delilah drew herself up to her haughtiest height—even from her seated position on the short stool. "My whereabouts are none of your concern."

It was worth a try, anyway.

Ravensworth nodded slowly, as if giving her words due consideration. "That is entirely true, but…"

Delilah waited, breath held, for him to finish the sentence. It was possible he was intentionally torturing her.

"But your whereabouts are your family's concern."

A point she couldn't argue—not that she owed this man an explanation. But her family…

It was quite simply that Amelia, Archie, and Juliet were now all happily married and settled and starting families. She couldn't always be hanging about—the unmarried spinster sister.

Delilah experienced the pang she always felt at the thought of Juliet—a pang of loss. Which was silly, really. Juliet hadn't died. She was alive and well in the wilds of the Scottish Highlands.

Her younger cousin by a year, Juliet had come to live with her uncle, aunt, and Windermere cousins after her parents had perished in a carriage accident. Juliet had been part of Delilah's life since before she'd begun forming memories. And since Juliet's marriage to one of the most wonderful men on the entire planet, Lord Rory Macbeth—a marriage Delilah didn't begrudge her cousin in the least—it simply felt that a sizeable portion of her heart held a void.

So, it only followed that after Juliet's elopement in April an idea would spring to mind. It was quite simple, really.

She didn't have to hang about.

She'd sought out the theater company that had been traveling through the area of Scotland where she and Juliet had been visiting and inquired about their summer schedule, which so happened to have them traveling south with the intention of arriving in London by fall.

It had been too perfect an opportunity and impossible to resist. From there, the invention of a Swiss friend and a yearning for some Alpine mountaineering had been a short hop. She'd joined Ye Olde Albion Players a few weeks later, thereby seizing the chance to run off for a summer. After all, just as her family had their own lives to lead, so, too, did she—a destiny to fulfill and her own happiness to pursue.

And she owed the man before her none of this explanation.

Yet...he didn't seem to understand that. "You cannot stay here, *Lady* Delilah," he said, smug, so certain of his rightness.

It was impossible to miss his emphasis on *lady*.

"*Shh*," she hushed, peering around him to make sure no one was within listening distance. "I'm Lilah here."

"*Lilah*," he repeated. Something flashed behind his eyes. If she didn't know better, she might think he liked that name for her.

And a responsive something flashed inside her, too—something that made deep, secret places slightly uncomfortable.

Something she'd felt before with this man, truth told. Something she always shoved to the side and ignored.

Like now.

"Do you think me too good for this life?" she asked.

His brow crinkled. "That's not what—"

"I'll have you know," she began, letting her righteousness flow. "The acting art is one of the most noble professions in all the world."

At that very moment, an actor dressed in a harlequin costume came to a stop before the open caravan doorway, just visible to the side of Ravensworth's rather massive form. The man gave a little wave and bow. Then on a quick, unexpected swivel, he presented his back, bent forward, and let rip the loudest, gustiest expulsion of wind anyone was ever likely to hear, before sauntering away, a satisfied swagger in his step.

Delilah only just didn't groan as she held a hand to her mouth to stem the sudden, riotous giggle that wanted out. Ravensworth lifted a single skeptical eyebrow. The high-in-the-instep duke crouched in a caravan doorway had likely never been subjected to such a blustery bit of flatulence in all his life.

Well, in all fairness, neither had she until she joined Ye Olde Albion Players. That harlequin got around.

She cleared her throat. "Windy actors, notwithstanding."

Ravensworth remained utterly unmoved. "Pack your belongings. You shall be coming with me tonight."

A statement of fact.

Delilah willed calm into mind and body before responding. She would get nowhere by fuming at the blasted arrogant man. "I understand that as a duke," she said, evenly, "you're accustomed to issuing edicts and having them followed, but *I* am not yours to command, and I shall do no such thing."

His jaw clenched and released, leaving a mulish set to his mouth.

It felt good to have put it there.

Then his golden eyes narrowed, and the solid ground shifted beneath Delilah's feet.

"Of course," he said, low and sure, "there is another solution."

"Which is?" she asked, wary.

"If you stay, I stay."

She searched his eyes for amusement within, for surely he was having her on. But it wasn't to be found. The breath caught in her chest. The man was utterly and completely serious. But...

He couldn't be.

He was bluffing.

"You wouldn't dare." She had nothing to lose by calling that bluff.

He didn't flinch. "I hear a carpenter is needed."

"A carpenter, yes," she allowed. "A duke, not so much." She canted her head. "In fact, I'm not sure what good a duke is in this world."

"Oh, I can think of a few things," he said. "A few of them I think you'd like very much."

The heat she'd experienced a few minutes ago sparked into a sudden conflagration.

Unspoken words lay between the spoken ones in that sentence.

She didn't understand.

No, that wasn't true.

She did understand. Men spoke words like that to women—to women they wanted to seduce.

Which was why she couldn't understand why *this* man had spoken those words to *her*.

"I'm a fair hand with a spanner," he said as if he hadn't just said that other thing.

She blinked. "A spanner?" What did a spanner have to do with anything?

"The tool."

"Ah."

He'd so upset the balance of what she'd thought was the basis of their acquaintance—her brother's closest friend...and her sworn enemy—that she'd momentarily forgotten what a spanner was.

She inhaled a bracing sip of air. "I'm staying through the end of summer."

There. That should set this conversation right.

"Then, so am I."

He simply stood, shoulder braced against the doorframe, arms crossed over his chest, looking utterly unmoved and utterly, damnably arrogant.

"Don't you have dukely responsibilities to take care of?"

He shrugged an indifferent shoulder. "My secretary can manage without me for a time."

Certainty sank deep into Delilah. "You're determined."

"Quite."

A roar of frustration wanted release. Why did this bloody duke always arrive to spoil her fun? Truly, it was a near universal constant in her life.

But she wasn't done fighting. "You're being absurd, of course. You can stop it now," she said, punching at a different angle. "You wouldn't dare join this troupe."

"Wouldn't I?"

She was starting to see how he and Archie were such good friends. While Archie proclaimed to the world his openness to a lark anywhere, anytime, Ravensworth kept that desire hidden—which didn't mean it wasn't there, lurking, just waiting for an opportunity.

Like this one.

Still, she couldn't give up. "You're a—" She lowered her voice. "*Duke.*"

He spread his hands wide as if that settled it. "See, there you have it."

But Delilah didn't see. Not at all. "*See? Have* what?"

She suspected she'd stepped into a trap.

"Dukes run around England doing whatever they please," he explained, patiently. "And *this*—running around England with a traveling theater company—pleases me. So, to your point, I would dare."

Delilah was struck speechless. Perhaps for the first time in her life.

"Further," he continued, "you're to tell the rest of the company that I'm a carpenter."

Ah. And here she had him. "Why in heavens name would I do that?"

"So I don't tell them you're a lady."

Of a sudden, Delilah felt like a popped balloon—all the air gone out of her in a great whoosh.

It was *he* who'd had *her* the entire time.

"This is most ungentlemanly behavior," she protested. It was worth a try.

"But I'm not a gentleman tonight—or for the foreseeable future." Ravensworth's sardonic smile went a little wicked. "You can call me Seb." A beat. *"Lilah."*

A shiver rippled through her at the velvet crush of her new name against his throat. She found her eyes straying down the strong column of that throat. Since working men didn't wear cravats, he wore only a neckerchief, leaving more of him open to view than his usual dukely self.

Seb.

She supposed a man like the one before her could be a Seb.

"Do you decree it, Your Grace?"

It would be dangerous to forget who he was.

She wouldn't let herself—no matter how appealing her gaze found the muscular column of his neck and the light brushing of hair peeking just above the V of his shirt.

Silently, he tipped his hat before pivoting on his heel and descending the caravan steps to disappear into the night.

But not from her life.

Quite the opposite, in fact.

It defied belief.

Ravensworth...

Her nemesis.

Here.

And yet...

Who was the man she'd just encountered?

She snorted. A man full of dukely imperative. And yet...

Tonight, dressed simply, he'd appeared all man...*manly*.

She'd never viewed Ravensworth as manly. *Handsome... sophisticated... arrogant... condescending...* Those were the insufferable ingredients that composed Ravensworth.

But, tonight—and presumably for the rest of the summer—he wouldn't be Ravensworth. He would be *Seb*.

And she would just have to suffer it.

She would ignore him.

It was possible.

Right?

The fact was she was under no obligation to spend time with Sebastian, the Duke of Ravensworth—or Seb the carpenter.

This summer was the start of the rest of her life.

And she wasn't about to let one meddling man—*duke!*—ruin it.

Not again.

Chapter Three

North Norfolk
A few weeks later

S EBASTIAN PROPPED A shoulder against a caravan wheel and turned the pasty in his hand every which way as he considered its solid, savory density and heft.

He'd never been much of a pasty man.

But after a few weeks of subsisting almost exclusively on the food, he was beginning to come around to its charms.

The other men taking their midday tea—Soppitt the head carpenter, Mattie the lad who handled the horses, Bran the farrier, and a man known simply as Fix-All—surely held no such observations. For these men, pasties were an ordinary, filling, tasty bit of midday sustenance.

Of course, as Sebastian tucked into the pasty he understood he'd never had the opportunity to view the reliable pasty in the way of these men. Not as the Duke of Ravensworth, anyway.

For the Duke of Ravensworth, every meal was a production. Meals held a cadence and a flow—a structure carefully choreographed by servants intent on keeping their positions in a duke's household through excellence of service and fare.

But, here, with the Albion Players, meals were simple and plain. In fact, he'd already developed a preference for this mode of eating. How many hours of his day as a duke did he waste filling his gullet? Somewhere between three to six, depending on his social calendar.

Too many.

He popped the last of the pasty into his mouth. Mutton, potato, and onion. A man didn't need much more than that.

He dusted the crumbs off his hands before wiping the remaining grease on his trousers. Something else the Duke of Ravensworth would never do.

He was rather taking to being Seb.

"Seb," came a voice.

Soppitt—the man Sebastian reckoned was his gaffer—jutted his black-stubbled chin, indicating a wagon at the opposite end of camp. "Now you're all finished up, fetch us that pile of timbers," he said. "And after that, you'll be repairin' the trap door on the stage, won't you?"

Sebastian gave a grunt in the affirmative.

He tried not to speak much, hence the grunting. And, actually, he'd found that a man needn't do much more than grunt to get his point across. In fact, a man could easily grunt his way through an entire conversation.

He knew because he'd been doing it these last few weeks.

He pushed off the caravan wheel and set to his task. It was a novel and slightly strange experience—this being told what to do, then doing it.

He began hauling the timbers, one by one, while the other men watched, making idle chit-chat and finishing their midday meal. This was yet another aspect he didn't mind about being a working man—the physical toil and sweat.

In the course of a duke's day, one found little opportunity to sweat. A duke had to seek it out. Horse riding...boxing... Those were good, sweaty pursuits. A good, long tup. Another good, sweaty pursuit.

In truth, it had been too long since he'd had one of those.

Not that there was any shortage of possibilities roaming the camp. He'd received no fewer than eight invitations from five different actresses to join her in her caravan bunk.

He'd always been aware of his effect on the opposite sex and had always assumed a sizeable part of his allure was his very large...*dukedom*. Other parts of him were large, too—he'd been informed on more than one occasion—but a dukedom trumped any parts of him having to do with being a flesh-and-blood man. He'd long accepted this as the way of the world, but here with the Albion Players, he was simply Seb.

Of course, there was one actress who he wouldn't mind if she sent an inviting—or even civil—glance in his direction, but she'd entirely stopped acknowledging his existence.

Lilah.

He liked that name for her.

It called to mind the Lady Delilah he'd known before The Eton Incident. A softer Delilah... A Delilah who had been friendly with him... A Delilah whose eye had occasionally directed a flicker of interest his way.

But that was Before. And for the last three years, they'd been living in the After, where she couldn't stand the sight of him.

Good deeds could certainly bring their own punishment.

Right.

He lifted another timber off the stack and for the hundredth time questioned exactly why he was here.

And for the hundredth time, the answer followed in an instant.

Keeping Delilah safe.

Again.

His task completed, satisfied sweat dripping down the sides of his face and the hollow of his spine, he rejoined the men, none of whom had shifted an inch in the last half hour. Life in a theater company moved at a different pace than what Sebastian was accustomed to.

"More than full of himself, that one," muttered Bran, just loud enough for the group to hear as an actor passed by. The man did possess a rather haughty angle to his dimpled chin.

The men, to a one, nodded their agreement.

Actors. A favorite subject of mild disdain amongst the men who kept the company running, if not in a smooth gallop, then at a serviceable limp, at least.

"And that Bliss…" began Fix-All.

Groans sounded around.

"If she summons me to her bunk again, like she's Queen Anne, I'll have to tell her what's what."

"And what's that?" asked Mattie, flashing a grin.

"It ain't the bed that got lumps in it, but her arse!"

This provoked more than a few guffaws.

Bran shrugged a shoulder. "I happen to like an arse with a few lumps in it. More cushion for the—"

"High of spirits, them actors," continued Fix-All, not one to be put off a subject. "Still, when Bliss did that scene as Lady Jane up there, it did bring an old bead of moisture to the eye."

Sebastian suspected Fix-All would be finding himself in Bliss's bunk tonight, after all.

Though a divide existed between the actors and the working men, each harbored a respect and admiration for one another's place in their special world. Neither could exist without the other.

A figure clambered up onto the stage, a sheaf of papers in her hand. *Tall… willowy… cropped blonde curls…*

Lilah.

Quiet descended as the men watched her pace the boards, her brow furrowed in concentration, her mouth moving silently as she went over her lines.

"And her?" Sebastian found himself asking.

Bran nodded. "That one's all right."

"Lovely as a sunrise, she is," offered Mattie.

"But not puffed up with it," added Soppitt.

Fix-All nodded pensively and tapped a forefinger to his chin in the pose of a philosopher. "A looker like that usually demands the lead. But not this one. She knows her place in the pecking order and respects it."

"I reckon she won't be happy with the bit parts for long," said

Soppitt. "She's too…" he trailed into silence.

She's too…

That summed up Delilah perfectly.

She was too *everything.*

"Anyone know where she came from?" asked Sebastian. It was time he knew the story she'd told.

Heads shook all around. "A mystery, that one," said Mattie, with no small amount of longing in his voice.

"I have a theory, meself," said Fix-All, lifting his brow meaningfully. "A high-born bastard."

The theory provoked a round of affirmative grunts.

"What makes you think that?" asked Sebastian.

"The way she talks and carries herself." Fix-All was clearly pleased at being asked to expand on his theory. "Like a lady. Tries to cover it up, though."

Soppitt's eye narrowed on Sebastian. "She talks a little like you, come to think on it."

"Yeah, well…" Sebastian trailed. Then he grunted, and that was the end of it.

Soppitt jutted his chin toward the stage. "The trap door isn't about to fix itself."

Sebastian nodded, even as he inhaled a snort. The Duke of Ravensworth didn't take too kindly to commands. But as Seb, well, he was able to shrug it off, because the work was only pretense, as far as he was concerned. The true reason he was here was currently pacing the boards, muttering to herself like a bedlamite.

He caught the very instant she registered his presence—not because she acknowledged him, but the opposite. Tension squared her shoulders, and she kept her gaze determinedly averted. He let his tools fall to the stage with a solid clank. Not even the flicker of a glance. That was how closely she was keeping the periphery of her eye on him.

"Lilah," he said.

She acted like she hadn't heard him and turned, presenting

him her back.

"You'll need to keep to that side of the stage while I repair the trap door."

She continued muttering to herself as if she hadn't heard him. But the tips of her ears betrayed her. They'd gone bright red. He suspected her cheeks had, too.

Arms crossed over his chest, he stared down at the gaping hole where the trap door should've been closed. Now, how to repair a trap door?

Right.

It wasn't anything a hammer, some nails, and the rusty spring Soppitt had placed in his hand couldn't fix.

He tossed Delilah one last glance before jumping into the gaping square hole. The stage now level with his chest, he considered the job before him. Nails had wormed loose from hinges that had rusted and curled from years of exposure to the elements and overuse. He considered the hammer, nails, and spring in his hand. He discarded the spring as useless. The solution was to employ a few cross boards and hammer the door shut until new hinges could be procured.

The Duke of Ravensworth decided it so.

The aristocrat in him wasn't buried so deeply, after all.

One last glance toward Delilah, who was intently keeping to her end of the stage, and Sebastian dropped to his knees and set about his task, through layers of cobwebs and much to the annoyance of a feral orange tabby cat who dashed away, but not before sending a few well-directed hisses his way.

But just as Delilah's person wasn't too far away, neither were thoughts of her.

He admired the seriousness with which she approached the craft of acting. Every evening, he'd watched her tread the boards. Though her parts were small, she never gave the same performance twice, acting intuitively, playing off the other actors and even the audience.

The fact was she shouldn't have been born a lady. If she

hadn't been, she would currently be reigning supreme over the finest stages of England and the Continent.

A stray wicked thought wormed in. *That Delilah* would've been in need of a patron. It wasn't that he wanted to collect her like a possession. But *that Delilah* might've been nice to him... Perhaps tossed a smile his way every so often... Given him a chance to...

He shouldn't finish the thought.

It decided to finish itself.

Seduce her.

He'd never been free to seduce Lady Delilah Windermere. But *Lilah*...

Well, she was an altogether different person.

Or she could be.

His forearm planted against the trap door above his head, holding it in place, he pinched a nail between forefinger and thumb and hammered it in place. One nail down, about forty to go if this fix was going to withstand two hours of stomping feet every night.

Right.

Truth told, he should reconsider this plan to travel with the company for the remainder of the summer. As he'd gotten to know the Albion Players, he saw that Delilah was perfectly safe here.

Further, he'd never seen her like this. She'd always been confident, but this Delilah—*Lilah*—was different. She not only knew what she was about, but she was capable. She didn't need her family name to thrive—and she certainly didn't need him to tell her what was good for her.

He hammered a nail in place, then another, and another. It was only when he took a rest from all the hammering—an activity that was surprisingly settling for the mind—that he realized he wasn't the one causing all the racket. Heels drummed on the boards near him... heels that advanced with a light, efficient *click-clack*... heels that didn't slow as they approached the half-secured trap door.

Sebastian was considering the possibility that he should move when a booted heel came down on the trap door, then the other. It was on the third step that the rickety contraption gave way, allowing him the split of a second to react as a body dropped into the hole. Though he was on his knees, his arms reactively shot out even as one of those booted heels planted itself in the center of his chest and kicked, knocking the wind out of him and shoving him onto his arse.

But gravity wasn't finished as the body continued its descent, crashing down on him as its landing cushion. Next thing he knew, he was flat on his back, a pair of long, slender legs straddling his chest, a woman's skirts flung over his face. His hands instinctively grabbed the woman's waist to steady her.

Except these weren't just any woman's skirts flung over his head.

They were Delilah's skirts.

Which made these Delilah's long, slender legs straddling him.

Delilah's womanly scent he was inhaling.

His cock went from still and unbothered to full and ready in an instant.

Frantic hands began shoving skirts aside. Over the hem, wide, startled azure eyes stared down into his.

Delilah's eyes.

Both speechless, their gazes remained locked…his hands clutching her waist…her cunny close enough to his face that all it would take for him to have a taste of her would be to pull her a few inches closer…

She swallowed, and his eyes followed the undulation of her elegant throat.

Here they were…

Not Ravensworth and Lady Delilah.

But Seb and Lilah.

Staring into each other's eyes longer than was strictly necessary.

And he wanted her with a ferocity he'd never once let himself experience.

Because he'd always known if he ever allowed himself to want her...

He would pursue her with the single-minded intensity that he pursued everything.

He wouldn't stop until he'd had her.

Chapter Four

A LONG WITH HER mind, Delilah's lungs refused to move. Both were decidedly stuck.

On the man below her.

She could hardly countenance where she was or how she'd gotten here. One moment she'd been pacing the stage and practicing her lines. The next, she was falling through the trap door, and now...

She was straddling Ravensworth, cobwebs in her hair, scratchy dirt beneath her knees.

Straddling Ravensworth.

That was the main point.

Good Lord.

It couldn't be...

She dragged her skirts back and confirmed that, yes, it was he. *His* solid, muscular chest below her. *His* hands clutching her waist. And *his* golden gaze staring up at her as intense and inscrutable as ever.

To be so centered within that gaze...

She couldn't move.

She'd never been this close to him.

She'd never known his scent.

Until now.

Citrus and cedar.

Lovely.

The man smelled lovely.

And the feel of him between her legs...

Lovely didn't come close to the correct word for that feeling.

Even as her mind rejected the very notion, her body experienced a very different response. As if the center of her had gone hot and liquid and needed—*oh*—needed to rub against something.

And the look in his eyes...

It said he could provide exactly that something.

Madness... This was utter and complete madness.

And yet she couldn't break away from it.

"Delilah," rasped against the back of his throat as his hands at her waist tightened and pressed her down upon him.

Her hips instinctively angled, and she gasped, suddenly supremely aware of a single fact. Only the fabric of his shirt lay between his muscled chest and...her—*oh*—sex...that sensitive flesh pressed against him, aching for...

He pulled her hips forward so *she* ground against him.

Sudden light sparked through her, and a little cry escaped her parted lips. His pupils flared as he moved her against him again, her thighs instinctively spreading wider. "Oh," she breathed.

What was happening?

She wasn't certain, but the man below her...

He was.

It was as if an awakening was occurring inside her, demanding she follow it, blind.

Again, she ground herself against him. This was madness. And yet she couldn't pull herself away. Deep, dark places inside her were coiling tight and making demands of her.

Demands she didn't know how to satisfy, though she must.

Or she would surely perish.

This time, her cry was one borne of frustration.

"Delilah," he spoke, his low, masculine voice vibrating below her. "I can give you what you want."

The part of her that must contradict his every word spoke up. "Because you always know best."

Oh, why had she said that?

Foolish woman.

"Let me touch you."

And she saw within his golden eyes, certainty.

He knew what she wanted.

And how to give it to her.

"Touch me," she demanded, asserting her right to have his touch upon her...*now.*

Long, capable fingers slid up her thigh, and a thin layer of perspiration sheened her skin. Immediately, she knew what had been missing as her eyes squeezed shut—*anticipating...craving...needing...*

His fingertip glided along her slit, and her eyes flew open, the breath freezing in her chest, as the coiling sensation in her sex pulled tighter.

A smile curled about his mouth. "So wet for me," he muttered.

Then that fingertip applied pressure to the sensitive flesh that only her own curious hands had encountered in the privacy of her bed.

But his finger caressing her *there—oh*—it was different...*better.*

That finger knew what it was doing as it rubbed her—her entire being centered in that exquisite half inch of flesh—her body collapsing forward, her hands planted on the ground to either side of his head, her face inches from his, his breath hot against her mouth, as he delivered a pleasure that swirled and looped, elusive, taunting...daring her to catch it. Then she managed to grab hold as a sudden burst seized her and exploded in bright light and molten sensation. The hand at her waist released and suddenly clapped over her mouth as she cried out, her quim pulsing against his fingertips.

And not once had his gaze left hers.

She could crumple atop him with satiety. But, at last, the instinct of self-preservation seized her, and she became acutely aware of...

Oh.

She was kneeling on the dirt beneath a stage straddling the Duke of Ravensworth, his long, capable fingers having just brought her to...

Oh.

What had she done?

Committed an act of supreme madness.

And she'd committed that act of supreme madness with...*Ravensworth.*

She scrambled off him and scuttled away on her bottom, panting for air as if she'd just sprinted fifty yards. "But you're my nemesis." Those were the first words out of her mouth.

His gaze pierced and searched hers, but it didn't flinch. "I've never been your nemesis, Delilah."

A head poked into the trap door opening. Soppitt, she thought his name was. "All right down there?"

Down there.

A blush began at the roots of Delilah's hair and crawled across her skin to her toes.

If only the man knew what he was asking.

"Just got the wind knocked out of me," said Ravensworth, pushing himself up and into a sitting position.

How coolly the lie rolled off his lips.

As if what had just happened hadn't just happened.

And it had most definitely happened.

Her quim that still tingled and throbbed with satisfaction could attest to the fact.

But how?

From start to finish, it couldn't have taken more than one—two?—minutes. She'd had no idea such a thing could be achieved in less than a minute—or that life could continue on after as if it hadn't.

All her life, she'd been called wild.

But this was the very first time in those four and twenty years that she'd truly acted on that impulse.

Wild.

Soppitt's hand reached down. "Lilah?"

She was meant to take it.

Which was just as well.

Distance from Ravensworth must be achieved...*tout suite.*

It occurred to her that in all the years she'd been acquainted with the man, she'd neither touched nor been touched by him.

And now she had been.

Intimately...

Thoroughly.

Delilah placed her hand in Soppitt's and allowed herself to be hauled up onto the stage. As she stood in the summer sunshine, slightly disoriented, her legs a bit wobbly, it was almost if dark, pleasurable happenings hadn't occurred below.

Almost.

Her body was having a decidedly difficult time pretending otherwise.

Her body... It had never felt like this before. Like she could feel the individual blood cells rushing through her veins.

Ravensworth appeared through the trap door opening, concentrated on the task of dusting off cobwebs and dirt, his dark blond hair tousled and mussed. He planted his hands on the stage and pushed himself up. Her gaze fell to those hands...his fingers, long and masculine.

Those fingers contained knowledge.

Like how to make her body feel like it did at this very moment—singing with light.

He twisted around so he came to a seat, his legs hanging through the trap door opening. He cleared his throat. Delilah's gaze startled up. She'd been staring at his hands.

The look in his arrogant golden eyes said he knew it.

And why.

"Lilah," came her name as if from a great distance.

She whipped around to find the company director Mr. Morgan three feet away, not thirty.

Ravensworth had her completely turned around and utterly muddled.

"Lilah," repeated Mr. Morgan in his Welsh lilt, handing her a sheet of paper. "Will you run these lines?"

Her gaze skated across the page. It was a scene from *Lover's Vows*. "I know the play well."

Her usual self began to return to her, even though she could feel the heat of Ravensworth's stare. That was nothing new. Every night, the first thing she did before a performance was locate him in the audience, so her gaze would never once happen that direction.

She took her place in the center of the stage and exhaled a long, steadying breath, inviting the docile, lovestruck spirit of Amelia, the heroine of *Lover's Vows*, to fill her. "Where would you like me to start, Mr. Morgan?"

"At the top."

Delilah glanced down and realized this was Act III. The scene between Amelia and Anhalt where they discuss matrimony and proclaim their love for one another. Her stomach churned. "Perhaps a different scene would be better." An idea came to her—a brilliant idea. "I don't have to play Amelia. I could play the Count." Then she wouldn't have any love scenes. *Perfect.*

Mr. Morgan flicked a dismissive wrist. "The audience would want you as Amelia."

Right.

Subtly, from beneath her eyelashes, she chanced a quick glance toward Ravensworth. Arrogant smile curled about his mouth, he was watching the proceedings with that intense, undivided attention of his.

She squeezed her eyes shut. This was an opportunity. Mr. Morgan was offering her the lead role in a scene—her first. She mustn't muck it up. She opened her eyes and spoke the line at the top. *"I will not marry."*

Mr. Morgan held up a hand and shook his head. "You need a scene partner." He cast his gaze about. No one happened to be around, other than—

His gaze landed.

Ravensworth.

Her heart became a hammer against her ribs.

No, no, no.

Mr. Morgan crooked his index finger. "My good man Seb, would you be so kind as to—"

"No!" burst from Delilah.

Both sets of eyes swung toward her, but Ravensworth was already pushing to his feet, unfolding all six feet and several inches of himself, that arrogant smile not having slipped a whit. He looked to be enjoying himself.

Of a sudden, Delilah saw Ravensworth, not as she'd seen him when she'd first met him as a friend of her brother's, but as if she were only seeing him now for the first time. The sheer physicality of the man. What she was seeing was what all the other ladies must've been seeing all these years. She felt slightly lost for breath.

Was this the effect he had on women? How had she been so oblivious to it?

She needed to get a firm grasp on herself.

The blasted man's effect on the opposite sex—or the fact that she might very well be included in that number—mattered not.

It didn't change what happened at Eton three years ago.

There, that was the ship righted.

Mr. Morgan ignored Delilah and pointed toward the stage boards. "Now, you'll stand here." That would have Ravensworth standing not three feet from her. She took a shuffling step backward. Mr. Morgan held up a halting palm. "Nay, you stay where you are, Lilah. These are lovers. They need to be close."

Delilah obeyed, but went as rigid as the boards beneath her feet. "I doubt he knows the lines." It was worth a try.

Mr. Morgan extended his copy of the play toward Ravensworth and pointed. "You'll start *there* after she begins."

Delilah sensed hesitation in Ravensworth, and for a hopeful moment, she thought he would exercise his dukely prerogative and refuse. Then he grunted his assent. He'd really taken to grunting since he'd joined the company.

Delilah understood two things at once. This was both her big chance and utterly impossible. But she understood something else, too. If she wanted to be treated like a lead actress, then she must act like one.

She cleared her throat and repeated her first line. *"I will not marry."*

What strange words to be saying in the general direction of Ravensworth. She held her gaze six inches to the right of his head, determined not to look directly at him.

He held his arm at a stiff angle and read out, *"You mean to say, you will not fall in love."*

"Oh no!" The next line wanted to stick in her throat. *"I am in love."*

Ravensworth might not know what direction this dialogue was taking—he was particularly fond of the high arts, and *Lover's Vows* certainly wasn't that—but she did.

"Are in love!" he proclaimed. *"With the Count?"*

Mr. Morgan held up a hand and stepped between them. "Lilah, this man is your one true love. You need to look at him, and perhaps caress your hand lovingly across his cheek. Give your words some *life*," he added with a dramatic flourish.

Even as she wondered if a slap counted as a loving caress, Delilah nodded and looked directly at Ravensworth—which was a mistake—for she immediately forgot her next line.

"I wish..." prompted Mr. Morgan.

"I wish I was," she said.

"Here, I have it," interrupted Mr. Morgan, stepping between Delilah and Sebastian and taking her hand. "Take *his* hand in *yours* and brush it across your cheek. Make Anhalt *feel* you,

Amelia."

"Pardon?" asked Delilah to buy some time. She'd never recovered her breath sufficiently, and here it was gone again.

"Like lovers do," explained Mr. Morgan.

Like lovers do…

Delilah's gaze fell to one inevitable destination. Ravensworth's hands. His left hand was the safer hand, of course. Less temptation in that hand. But her eye would stray toward his right hand and those long, knowledgeable fingers. Fingers that minutes ago had…

She squeezed her eyes shut. This was supposed to have been the summer of her dreams. Instead, thanks to one breathtakingly arrogant man, it was turning into the summer of her nightmares.

But she wanted this role. How badly? She reached for his hand—*oh*…the right one—and placed it on her cheek. A scent hit her nose. Musky…

Her.

Then she made her second mistake. She looked up…and directly into his intense golden eyes. How had she never noticed the flecks of green?

And his scent of cedar and citrus… Here it was again.

On a few occasions, she'd imbibed more than a wise amount of wine with dinner. The feeling stealing through her now was exactly like that. And it was *Ravensworth* who provoked it…

It was all entirely too much to grasp in the ten minutes since…

Oh.

What a thought to finish.

"Lilah," said Mr. Morgan, "start at *why so?*"

Delilah stared into Ravensworth's green-flecked golden eyes, the feel of his calloused palm sliding along her cheek toward the nape of her neck, his long fingers weaving through her hair… The banked strength of a man… She'd never experienced it before— how it made a woman feel. Her eyes wanted to drift half closed…her body to follow the subtle tug of his hand forward—

"Lilah, that'll be all," said Mr. Morgan.

Delilah's eyes flew wide. "The scene's not finished."

"But we are," Mr. Morgan tossed over his shoulder, already halfway across the stage. "Let's try again next week once you've had a little more time on the stage under your belt. Stage fright gets everyone at the beginning."

Delilah had never once experienced stage fright in her life. She was opening her mouth to say exactly that, but Mr. Morgan was already gone, his usual tuneless whistle trailing in his wake.

Helpless frustration replaced whatever other feeling that had been coursing through her moments ago. She'd allowed precious opportunity to slip through her fingers. And why?

Because of the man standing before her with an assessing, cocked angle to his head.

She only just realized she was still holding his hand, which was now fully cradling her head, angling her face up, her mouth only inches from his...so close all she had to do was lift onto her toes to know the taste and texture of his lips...

Then she remembered she was damned angry at this man.

With one giant, ungainly step backward, she broke the contact—and the spell he'd cast over her. "It would be best if you stayed away from me for the rest of the summer." Even as the words passed her lips, her body cried out in protest.

Well, one part of her body.

He nodded slowly. "I can do that, but..."

"But?"

"Can you stay away from me?"

The arrogance of the man!

"Of course I can stay away from you," she scoffed.

A single eyebrow lifted. In case she'd forgotten he was a duke. "You think so?"

"Of course," she repeated with growing certainty.

"Even after..." he trailed.

"*Even after?*"

Oh, why was she still standing here? Why was she allowing

him to continue?

They both knew *even after* what.

And to speak it aloud...

Well, no good could possibly come from that.

"Even after you've had a taste of what I can give you."

There went her breath again. "A taste?" she asked without thinking. It wasn't her mind asking the question.

His smile went more than a little wicked. "Oh, there's more." A beat. *"Much."*

And with that, he pivoted on his heel and strode—possibly swaggered—off the stage, leaving Delilah alone.

Nay, not alone. She had his last word to keep her company. *Much.*

And the certainty it would plague her dreams tonight.

Chapter Five

A week later

DELILAH ROUNDED A bend in the footpath she'd been ambling along for the last ten or so minutes and was met full in the face with a blast of early-morning sea breeze lifting straight off the ocean. Her hair, curls unbound, whipped about her as she picked up the scent of salt on the air, the taste of it on her lips.

The rising sun was a red fireball in the east as hazy gray clouds hovered above the far-away horizon, catching and absorbing the light, then sending bright rays streaking across the sky, above and below. And beyond them, directly above her head, the sky hung gray-blue, even as a placid gray-blue sea mirrored it below; small, uniform waves meeting the soft, mellow sand of the shore with a muted roar in the morning quiet.

She stopped and unlaced her boots before kicking them off entirely. Her cotton stockings quickly followed. She wanted to feel the night-cool sand between her toes. Today was the Albion Players' last day on the coast before they cut inland. Everyone had the day on their own, and instead of performing tonight, the company would light a bonfire on the beach.

It felt a bit pagan to Delilah, and she couldn't wait.

She stuffed her stockings into her boots and tied the laces together, before slinging them over her shoulder. She cut left, venturing off the path and striking out across the sand dunes toward the shore. She was half sliding down one, hands out, trying to keep her balance when she noticed a figure in the water. Not a sea animal, but an animal of the human variety, out from the shore about twenty yards, one arm after the other slicing through the water in smooth rhythm, swimming like he had somewhere to go.

He.

Yes, definitely a *he*, judging by the broad expanse of his back and shoulders, the bulk and cut of muscles on his arms, his dark blond hair just grazing his shoulders...

A ping of recognition spiked through her.

This wasn't any *he*—but the *he* she'd been avoiding this last week.

Ravensworth.

Swimming at dawn.

Her eyes narrowed on one particular point in the water.

His taut, white, *naked* arse.

Ravensworth wasn't simply swimming in the ocean at dawn.

He was swimming in the ocean at dawn, *naked.*

Her feet started moving—not away, but *toward.*

She should bolt in the opposite direction. But when had she ever resisted the call of a provocation? To do so now went against her very nature, and this summer adventure was about being entirely herself and following her interests and passions.

And the Duke of Ravensworth? How did he fit into the context of her interests and passions?

He didn't, of course. Still, it was a question better left unexamined after...oh, after what happened a week ago.

Something else better left unexamined.

Except her body remembered—too well.

Last night, she'd placed her own hand *there*, as her body had been craving, the ache having become too much. But it wasn't the same, and instead of pleasure, she'd only delivered herself disappointment.

But Ravensworth—the man she'd spent the last three years despising...the man whose naked arse held the entirety of her attention—he knew how to deliver.

He'd awakened her.

And though she shouldn't, she wanted more.

At the bottom of the dune, she spotted a dark mass and slid the rest of the way toward it. A pile of clothes, folded neatly. They could belong to none other than Ravensworth.

Impulsively, she lowered to a seat squarely atop the neat pile and stared out to sea, luxuriating in the feel of sand sliding between her toes, becoming mesmerized by the small waves lapping the shore, the rhythmic slice of his arms through water that couldn't be much warmer than this side of frigid.

She felt the sudden impulse to strip off all her clothes and join him, but quickly decided it was an impulse better left ignored.

The truth was she wasn't as impulsive as people thought. She took careful consideration before acting. But it was simply her inclinations tended toward the unconventional, which made them easy for others to dismiss as wild and flighty.

But she was neither of those things. She simply wanted a life fashioned and forged by her own hand and talents.

And this summer she'd found it.

She couldn't help wondering if now that she'd gotten a taste for freedom, she could leave it behind in a month.

After a good long while, Ravensworth switched direction and cut toward the shore...swimming directly toward her.

Every muscle in her body tensed with sudden anticipation. She was sitting on his clothes...effectively holding them hostage. That would tweak his nose. It wasn't too late to jump to her feet and leg it down the trail back to her caravan.

Yet she remained silent and still.

"Can you stay away from me?"

He'd put the question to her a week ago.

And she had stayed away.

Until now.

Until she'd sat on his clothes, watching his naked form slice through the water.

Not staying away.

The fact was she wanted to tweak him. She wanted to test him. She wanted to see him react to her provocation.

His head lifted to scan the shore, and her heart began racketing about her chest. Then his golden gaze found her and his forward momentum came to a sudden halt. It was the first time she'd met his eyes in days—since…

Since *a week ago* was a fact established.

The *why* of it, too.

No need to cover that ground yet again.

"What precisely are you doing, Lilah?" he called out, treading water.

Lilah. She hadn't given him leave to call her by that name. But he didn't need it—not when he was simply Seb.

"Enjoying the glory of the sunrise," she responded, unable to control a grin. *"Seb."*

The muscles of his neck and shoulders glistened with seawater and morning sun.

She couldn't help noticing.

"Seated atop my clothes?" he asked, the question not a question at all.

She shrugged. This was fun. "They're truly perfectly placed."

"I'll be needing them presently."

Truly, she shouldn't smirk. "When I'm ready."

Who didn't enjoy exerting a little power over a duke?

His eyebrows lifted, and even across this distance she caught a light enter his golden eyes—*challenge.*

An unhurried smile slid across his mouth, and a long, slow shiver purled up her spine. She'd only thought to taunt him, but it was occurring to her that she'd crossed an invisible line and had thrown down the gauntlet.

And he'd accepted.

He began swimming forward.

Toward shore.

Toward *her.*

She watched, mouth dry. She simply couldn't retreat from her position. But how could she possibly hold it?

She noted the instant his feet caught purchase on the bottom. Her stomach tightened as he began to emerge from the sea; one slow, relentless step after another, all golden and glistening like the sort of god people once worshipped.

And Delilah could see why.

The muscles of his shoulders, chest, and ridged stomach created channels for water to stream, leading the eye like gravity, *down...down...down...*

"You wouldn't dare," she called out, futilely. It was obvious that he was, indeed, daring.

How was it that his smile became even more arrogant?

The shiver spread and rippled through her.

"Watch me."

Watch him?

How could she look away?

"Of course," he continued, "you won't."

"Why would I?" she asked in a disinterested show of bravado. Hopefully, he hadn't detected the slight wobble in her voice.

He shook his head chidingly. "That's not the question. Would you dare *not* look away?"

Delilah's mouth snapped shut to prevent it gaping open. There were no words as he moved through the water, and she stared, transfixed, at the Adonis emerging from the sea.

Or would that be Poseidon?

Oh, what did it matter?

What did anything else possibly matter?

The water reached his waistline. Heat flushed across her skin. She should lift her gaze and keep it fixed above his neck—simply to prove to him that she could.

And herself.

Really, she should fix her gaze upon any point other than where it insisted on landing.

Another step. A fuzzy mound of golden hair revealed. Her

heart beat hard and fast against her ribs, and she had the strangest sensation of floating outside her body. *Yet another step...*

And there he was in his full morning glory. His thick thighs...his—*oh*—manhood. So visceral and masculine.

Ravensworth.

Before her was no duke of girlish fantasy, but a flesh and blood man.

She'd spent so many years despising Ravensworth that he'd become like a villain in an uninspired play—flat and possessed of a single dimension. But these last few weeks—*here...now*—she was able to see him fully, as the man he was.

The sand continued to shift beneath her feet—and not simply of the literal variety.

Ravensworth wasn't simply daring her to look at his naked form.

He was daring her to look upon him fully—as the man he was.

Which would require her to see him—all of him.

A realization that had caught her sideways a week ago—and again now.

Was she ready to see him in that way?

The feeling snaking through her body, making her thighs squeeze together, suggested she was.

Waves lapping at his ankles, he stepped from the shoreline and strode across the sand. He ran a hand through his hair, loosing droplets of sea water, slicking his hair back, though one lock insisted on flopping across his forehead. He radiated the confidence of a duke—of a man aware of his supreme attractiveness.

It should've been off-putting.

It wasn't.

The arrogant smile on his mouth...

That should've been off-putting, too.

It, too, wasn't.

His dukely arrogance only enhanced his devastating good

looks.

As he neared her, she knew she should shoot to her feet and make for the dunes. Yet her body refused to obey. She glanced away. It was like staring at the sun. One had to avert one's gaze at some point, or risk having brilliant light imprint itself permanently onto one's eyes.

She'd been risking precisely that with Ravensworth just now.

She suspected, however, it was already too late. He may have already permanently imprinted himself onto her.

He reached her side, and—*oh, Lord*—she dare not glance up, instead presenting him with her profile, her gaze fixed, unseeing, on the horizon. But what she saw at the edge of her vision...that was another matter.

He crouched beside her. "Lilah," rumbled low in his chest.

"Hmm?" She didn't have to unclench her jaw to make the utterance.

Below the scent of salty ocean traced citrus and cedar—*him*.

She caught it in her lungs and didn't let it go for the span of a dozen rapid heartbeats, even as her left cheek blazed beneath the heat of his gaze.

"If you wouldn't mind," he said, the low murmur quaking through her. She felt a tug below her bottom.

Then she understood.

She was still holding his clothes captive.

And he wanted them back.

So he could dress himself.

Right.

She shifted to the side, and he slid the folded pile from beneath her. Indirectly, she watched him dress. Fustian trousers sliding up long, muscled legs. Efficient fingers buttoning the fall. Brown homespun slipping over his head. A quick tuck of the shirt into the waistband of his trousers.

Not yet fully dressed, but made decent enough for delicate, feminine eyes, she darted a glance toward him as he lowered to a seat beside her, his shoulder just not touching hers as they stared out to sea, side by side.

His proximity made her oddly nervous, as if the blood in her veins had a life of its own.

"I must admit I'm a little disappointed," he said.

"And why is that, Your Grace?" She needed the distance his title provided.

"You didn't attempt to extract a ransom for my clothes."

"And what should my price have been?" she somehow asked.

He shifted to face her, his intense golden gaze landing on her to devastating effect.

Her lungs forgot how to breathe.

Her heart forgot how to beat.

This man... What was he doing to her?

Actually, that wasn't the question on her body's mind.

It was more concerned with what he presently *wasn't* doing to her.

AWARENESS CRACKLED THROUGH the air.

It occurred to Sebastian that he could reach out and take the nape of Delilah's neck in his hand, his fingers sliding through silky blonde curls, and draw her forward.

The look in her eyes suggested she wouldn't offer resistance.

But was that what he wanted for their first kiss?

First kiss.

A word that suggested that if there was one kiss, then another would surely follow.

But he wanted more from a Delilah kiss than a lack of resistance.

He wanted her to feel as if she would die without it.

He wanted an enthusiastic *yes*.

And while she might be close, she wasn't quite there yet.

So, he snorted.

Her eyebrows crinkled together, and she blinked as if released from a trance. She also looked slightly disgruntled. Then she sniffed, and her gaze shifted toward the sea. "We cut inland tomorrow."

Was this Lady Delilah Windermere making small talk? He hadn't known her capable of it. He supposed he could play along, even as a pang of disappointment shot through him.

He should've kissed her.

And now the moment was lost.

"Aye," he said, the syllable emerging on a grouchy note.

"And the bonfire tonight," she continued. "Will you be attending?"

Ah. So it wasn't small talk. "Why do you ask?" he asked, knowing exactly why, but wanting her to say it anyway.

She shrugged a shoulder.

"So you can decide whether or not to come yourself?" He wasn't truly asking.

Her lips twitched as if deciding whether or not to smile—or frown. "Possibly."

He chuckled. He couldn't help himself. One thing he'd always appreciated about this woman: she was honest. "If you must know," he said, "I'll be collecting wood for the bonfire and helping construct it, so I shall, indeed, be in attendance."

She released a deep sigh. "I didn't have you down as one to involve himself in pagan beach happenings."

"Well, Lady Delilah, you don't know me at all."

It had to be said.

Incredulous eyes swung his way. "I've known you for well over a decade. What a ridiculous thing to say."

He shook his head. Though sand shifted beneath his arse, firm ground stood beneath his feet. "You've been acquainted with the Duke of Ravensworth, I'll grant you that."

"You *are* the Duke of Ravensworth."

"That was the title I was given from the moment of my birth. Should I list all my other titles for you?"

"What exactly are you getting at?"

"The titles don't make the man."

She blinked, slowly. "You are the Platonic ideal of all that is Ravensworth. Who are you if you're not him?"

"Seb, builder of beach bonfires and enactor of pagan happenings. But my point is, aren't you curious about who I am? Who I *truly* am?"

A question she wasn't ready to answer. He could see it in her eyes. She wanted him to be Ravensworth. So she could keep him tidy and contained within a single dimension.

All because of what happened at Eton.

In that moment, he decided. The time had arrived to have the truth of that day out between them.

He was opening his mouth to do precisely that, when she opened hers first. "About what happened," she said. A light blush pinked her cheeks.

Though it sounded like a continuation of his own thoughts, she wasn't speaking of Eton. Only one happening could provoke that particular blush… Their, erm, *tête-a-tête* beneath the stage.

"You'll have to be more specific." He wouldn't be helping her with this.

She opened her mouth, closed it, then opened it again. "You don't have any regrets for, erm, *it?*"

Regrets?

Was the woman mad?

"No," he stated. It was the simple truth.

"*No?*"

He gave his head a slow shake. "Do you?"

"That's not a question a gentleman would ask."

She was evading.

He wouldn't let her. "Lilah," he began.

"I haven't given you leave to call me Lilah," she said, the picture of primness—except for her bare feet and the subject at hand.

He snorted. "May I call you Lilah?"

"You're going to anyway," she groused.

"True." He caught her gaze and held it. "Here's what you need to understand."

"What?"

"I brought you pleasure, and to express regret for that would be a lie."

"Oh."

The awareness that ever simmered between them heated up by a degree.

Again, here was that urge to reach out and pull her close and press his mouth to hers.

But he kept his hand still at his side.

She bit her bottom lip between her teeth and released it. A new light shone in her eyes. One he'd only observed from a distance. This light had never been directed at him...until a week ago.

And now, again.

A wild light.

"You never told me what my price for the return of your clothes should've been," she near whispered.

Why was she pushing this—pushing *him*? For the knowledge of his unanswered price shone in her eyes.

Then it occurred to him—walloped him over the head, really. Here she was, voicing *desire*.

Here was her enthusiastic *yes*.

She wanted to pay the price.

He lifted his hand and slid his fingers through short, loose curls around to the nape of her neck. He angled forward, invading her space, so his mouth was only a whisper's breath away. *"This."*

Sweet.

That was his first impression of Delilah.

Her lips tasted of summer sunshine and fresh strawberries and salt picked up from the ocean breeze.

She tasted of everything he'd ever wanted in a kiss.

He swiped his tongue across her bottom lip. She gasped, then smiled against his mouth. She liked that. He did it again, and her tongue ventured out to meet his, its tip sliding across his lower lip, tangling with him.

Of course, these weren't the first lips of Delilah's that he'd experienced.

His cock, which had been at half-mast since he'd first spotted her in the dunes, went hard as stone.

And so, too, had those lips been wet.

He pulled her closer on a growl.

He'd never growled in his life.

But he was now.

For Delilah.

He caught the curve of her waist and tugged, and she released a sigh into his mouth as she swayed forward. A rational thought pushed through the haze of desire fogging his brain. If he went further with this kiss—crushed her body against his...felt her cherry-hard nipples through the muslin of his shirt—there would be no turning back.

No turning back for him.

No turning back from Delilah.

But perhaps he'd already passed that point.

Perhaps he'd passed it years ago.

Of a sudden, her eyes flew open, as if she'd followed the flow of his thoughts and had come to the same realization. But had arrived at a different conclusion, if the panic in those blue depths was a fair indicator. The next instant, she broke away and pushed off his chest, scrambling back a good five feet. He seemed ever to have that effect on her. Her fingers touched lips swollen from the kiss.

"Was the price too high?" he asked.

What was this need ever to provoke her?

On a strangled cry, she shot to her feet.

"I'll take that as a *yes*."

With another strangled cry, she whirled around and began clambering up the dune.

As he watched her manage to somehow slip and slide *up* the

dune—no mean feat, that—a realization landed on Sebastian. He was having quite a few of those lately. This realization was one he hadn't allowed to occur to him in all these weeks of traipsing around England in Lady Delilah Windermere's wake.

No longer was he waiting for her to come to him.

He was actively pursuing her.

And she seemed to be meeting him somewhere near halfway.

Surprising, that.

He pushed to his feet and began following her, keeping her in his sights as they returned to camp. Whatever it was happening between them would go no farther than halfway if they didn't have it out about Eton.

He realized that, too.

Simply, he didn't want her to despise him anymore. Perhaps she would still despise him after he told her how and why events had transpired the way they had. But then, at least, she would despise him with all the correct information.

And, perhaps, she would stop despising him altogether.

He didn't expect her to rush into his arms, proclaiming him her savior. But it would be nice if she desisted stabbing him with random murderous glares. Like the one she'd just thrown over her shoulder as they entered camp.

His instinct was to follow her to her caravan and have it out between them now. But two reasons stopped him.

First, the other two actresses sharing the caravan with her. Last time he'd happened upon Flora and Dorie they'd suggested each taking a turn having their way with him. Actually, it had sounded more like a promise than a suggestion.

And then there was Soppitt pointing a finger at him. The Duke of Ravensworth would've flicked away such a summons like a gnat off his sleeve. But Seb couldn't. Not if he wanted to continue on in the company.

Not if he wanted to pursue matters with Delilah.

Right.

His feet switched direction. The time had arrived for him to start building a bonfire. Besides, a good stretch of honest toil was exactly what he needed.

Something—*anything*—to take his mind off Delilah.

Tonight.

Tonight he would have it out with her, and put an end to a past that would block some sort of future.

And while he wasn't sure of that future, he had an inkling of what it might hold.

As flimsy as that *might* was, it held enough substance to impel him forward.

Chapter Six

Later

ONLY AFTER NIGHT had descended fully, settling onto the countryside like a black cloak, the stars faraway twinkling pinpricks of light, did Delilah step foot from her caravan.

She was the last of the company to venture out, the distant sounds of revelry told her, even as she felt it in the stillness of camp.

Reputation cast her as the boldest and wildest of the Windermere brood—and her reputation had it half right.

She was bold.

She was wild.

But only recently.

That was what no one truly understood about her. What she hadn't truly understood about herself until a few days ago...

And again this morning.

And it was Ravensworth—of all people—who was bringing out her true audacity.

She didn't like it.

That wasn't precisely true.

She didn't *want* to like it—which was an altogether different matter.

Which was why she'd been sorely tempted to stay in her caravan tonight, pretend sleep, and skip the bonfire.

Because *he* would be there.

To call to her boldness and wildness.

But she couldn't. The pull of a pagan bacchanal on the beach was too irresistible to miss. Already her feet were moving in step to the strains of fiddle music drifting on the breeze.

So it was that soon those same feet were treading down the path from this morning, music and laughter pulling her along, the orange glow of the bonfire growing brighter with every step. She was dressed simply, white muslin shirt tucked into the waistband of a plain homespun skirt with only a shawl to keep encroaching night cool at bay. She'd left her shoes in the caravan.

Dirt and grass turned to sand beneath her bare feet and soon she was ascending the short rise of a dune. She reached the top, and the view opened to her. It was a beach utterly transformed from the one that had been quiet with morning stillness—where she'd held a duke's clothes hostage and all but begged him to kiss her.

Scattered across the beach were the Albion Players. A grouping over here joined arm in arm as they sang a bawdy sea shanty. The company's fiddler over there striking bow across strings much to the delight of those inclined toward dancing, trouser legs rolled above knees, skirts tucked into waistbands, allowing bodies freedom to dance and dance and dance. Some arms were linked, others swayed in the air, as feet moved round the bonfire that crackled and roared and spread glorious heat and light at the heart of it all, bright red sparks ascending toward the heavens above.

Here, anyone could be naught more than simple human being, taken by the call of the night.

Here, she was able to see England in a way she never had before. An England free of the rigid mores and rules of the *ton*.

Free.

Somehow, she'd come to inhabit a world where life was fun. She was a Windermere, and true to her birthright she always looked for—and found—the fun. In London, though, fun never felt safe. Fun felt more akin to walking a tight rope at a high altitude, all eyes watching...waiting...hoping for a fall, either from malice or simply for something to gossip about because the boredom ran so deep.

Yet here, on a wild stretch of Norfolk shore, fun was safe.

She was halfway down the sand dune when a hand reached for hers. It belonged to the cook's son. Lanny, he was called. He couldn't have more than eleven years on him. On a laugh, she allowed him to take her hand and lead her into the scrum of dancing—bodies carefree and gyrating and sweating. Though a head shorter than her, he twirled her around. On another laugh, she ducked under his arm and her hesitancy fell away as she gave over to the dance that had no set movement or pattern. One's feet and arms simply followed where the heart and inclination led. Someone shoved a mug into her hand, and she drank deeply of its contents. *Mead.* On a usual night, it would be too sweet for her tastes, but tonight it was perfect. She took another long swig.

Every now and again, her eyes cast about—beyond the other dancers, beyond the bonfire. As much as she might try to tell herself she wasn't looking for *him*, she was.

She knew it every time she felt a pang of disappointment when she didn't find him.

Then, soon, she knew it when her heart jumped into a gallop when she did.

There, standing at the edge of flickering bonfire light, was Sebastian with a small group of other company men, giving them the entirety of his attention as he always did when in conversation. Lit by the flickering glow of the bonfire, he was laughing and talking, the breeze lifting off the ocean tousling his hair about. In the weeks since he'd joined the company, his hair had grown longer, curling at the ends, catching the sun in light blond streaks. The man was simply gorgeous and glorious.

In all the years she'd known him, how had she never noticed?

She hadn't allowed herself to, that was how. He'd been Archie's close friend, and then her nemesis.

And yet...this Ravensworth—*Seb*—he was utterly unlike that version of Ravensworth—the one she'd had in her mind all this time.

Seb.

He had a good reputation with the other players, and more than a few of the women more than admired him. And today, he'd pressed his mouth to hers. His tongue had licked her bottom lip, and lit places inside her aflame that she hadn't known existed.

And all she could think as she watched him converse with those other men was that she wanted to drag him into the dunes and make him do it again.

Seb...Ravensworth...

The man who was her nemesis. And yet...

Something about that didn't feel right.

"I've never been your nemesis, Delilah."

Those had been his words beneath the stage. But it wasn't simply the words that had been haunting her since. It was the sincerity with which he'd spoken them.

He no longer *felt* like her nemesis.

And she wondered now if his words were true—that he never had been. And if so, how was that possible?

What was she missing?

One of the men in his group—she believed the man went by, improbably, *Fix-All*—must've said something particularly funny, for Ravensworth threw his head back on a laugh. She'd never seen him laugh like that—with abandon.

Then his gaze shifted and caught hers. No waver of surprise in those golden, moss-flecked depths. As if he'd known all along that she'd been observing him, and he'd let her take her fill. His smile didn't altogether fall away, but turned quiet and assessing. It wasn't a smile for his compatriots.

It was a smile for her.

He took a step, and she did, too.

Surely, slowly, they began walking toward each other, the hold of their gazes never wavering, the space between them nonexistent now that they'd locked eyes. It occurred to Delilah that, perhaps, it had ever been so.

For all the years she'd known him, a spark of awareness had lit through her whenever he entered a room. She'd never needed to look directly at him to know exactly where he was. It was an instinctive awareness. But it was more, too.

A *pull*.

A pull that didn't feel rooted in dislike or enmity, but something else—something less tangible.

Could it be the opposite?

Could it be that she *liked* him?

Or perhaps *like* had nothing to do with what drew her to him?

Did a magnet have to like the object it was drawn to?

It simply was.

Elements colliding.

Her gaze fell to his mouth, the remembered feel of it against hers—*firm... possessive... capable...*

Oh, yes, this man was certainly capable, and her body demanded to know what more he was capable of.

They stopped a few feet from one another, firelight catching the sharp angle of a cheekbone, the strong line of his jaw, the blond streaks in his hair...the intention in his eyes... A shiver traced through her, and she felt suddenly awkward and shy of him. He was all man, and she wasn't sure what to do with Ravensworth the man.

But one fact was certain: he knew precisely—*deliciously*—what to do with Delilah the woman.

He reached out, and without hesitation, she allowed his long, masculine fingers to twine through hers. No question that she wouldn't. He pulled, and the distance between them closed as she swayed forward, sand shifting beneath her feet, sliding between her toes. His other hand closed about her waist, and her head tipped back, their mouths—mouths that had touched only hours ago—inches from each other. All she would have to do was lift onto the tips of her toes to—

He shifted closer, but his mouth cut left and found the whorl of her ear. "May I have this dance, Lilah?"

Lilah... She was Lilah, and he was Seb. *Tonight.* How seductive an idea...

"Yes," she whispered, breathless, against his neck, catching his scent. *Citrus and cedar.* Something else, too. *Sweat.* From building the bonfire, no doubt. A complex, musky scent that provoked a response—the elemental pull that was becoming quickly familiar. Now that she was able to see it, she was coming to grasp it.

He pulled her closer, and she pressed herself against the hard, unyielding length of him. As their feet began to move, she knew why, for she'd seen the proof only this morning. Muscles that bulked his arms and shoulders, chest and stomach, thighs and calves. She'd heard Archie mention Ravensworth's penchant for the boxing ring, and here beneath the hand that rested on his shoulder she felt the consequence of that pursuit.

She gave a reflexive squeeze, and humor lit within his eyes. "Like what you feel?"

Her mouth opened, poised to speak the truth. *Yes.* She very much liked what she felt.

Or did she?

Because she felt with more than her hands.

A feeling had been coursing through her for days now—a feeling of restlessness and want and need—that he'd provoked, and she wasn't sure she liked it at all.

Because it was he who provoked it.

The man she'd long considered her nemesis.

How could she possibly like it?

And yet...

She suspected she did.

Matters as they stood could no longer hold between them.

"I need to know," she found herself saying into the space between their mouths.

"Yes?" rumbled from him.

"Why did you do it?"

)℅

SEBASTIAN DIDN'T NEED to ask Delilah to clarify the question.

She wasn't speaking of their kiss.

Or the interlude beneath the stage.

She was speaking of Eton.

She was asking why he'd exposed her.

He released her waist, but held on to her hand and led her through the bacchanal of raucous singing and laughing and dancing bodies. Past the edge of light, their eyes adjusted to the dark as they made their way along the beach and around a bend to a snug, sandy cove populated by only them, music and laughter echoing in the far distance.

He shed his coat and spread it flat, just out of reach of the shoreline, before extending a hand and gesturing for her to take a seat. Once settled, she glanced up and patted the remaining patch of cloth beside her—an invitation.

He accepted, angling himself so he could look out to sea, but also keep an eye on her. She was watching him expectantly, waiting for him—to explain his past self.

Best to start at the very beginning. "I'd received an invitation to visit my old stomping ground of Eton College," he said. "On the surface, it was to celebrate some anniversary, but the real reason was to inveigle funds from me for a new arts wing. A game I know well." He snorted. "I may have invented it."

Delilah canted her head. "How many arts wings have your name emblazoned on them, anyway?"

His eyes screwed up. "Eight? Nine?" He shrugged. "One loses count."

Delilah snorted. "Not one for false modesty, are you?"

"I'm not," he returned. "I'm a duke. It would be disingenuous."

Her teasing smile slipped into one more considering.

He needed her to understand something about him. *"Patron of the arts* is the role I've carved out for myself in society. It's my privilege, too—shaping the artistic tastes of England."

A note of mischief entered Delilah's eye. "And here I thought you were a lech who was only in it for the mistresses."

He accepted the teasing. She wasn't entirely wrong. "I won't deny there have been a few opera singers along the way, but that's not my primary, or even secondary, motivation. I'm sure you know that many are fooled into thinking bad art is good art. But through patronage, I have placed myself in the position to ensure good art wins."

"What? You're the self-appointed art god? The Zeus of the arts?" she asked, not without a little scorn. "Art is subjective. Why is it for you to decide what's good and what isn't? People like what they like."

She wasn't wrong—but she wasn't altogether right, either. "But you must allow that what's popular isn't always good." He would take it a step further. "In fact, it's often bad."

"You are truly a snob," she said, incredulous. "You know that, don't you?"

He wasn't here to make excuses for himself. So, he continued with the plain truth. "I cannot tolerate the idea of an artist possessed of genius slipping through the cracks of obscurity. Not when I have the means to do something about it."

The expression on Delilah's face as she took in his words... He'd never seen it—at least, not directed at him. *Respect.* "You're so..."

Her brow crinkled as she searched for the correct word. Sebastian's hands clenched at his sides, fingernails biting into his palms, as he waited.

"Responsible."

A laugh escaped him. No small amount of relief in that laugh. "I'll take that as a compliment."

"It is."

The way her azure gaze was taking him in, as if she were only now seeing him for the first time... Sebastian felt suddenly winded, as if an arrow had struck dead center in his chest. He could easily veer off course here—the largest part of him wanted to—but to do so wouldn't serve his larger purpose. For tonight—this moment—wasn't about immediate gratification. It was part of a longer game.

A game he was playing to win.

Though she didn't know it yet.

She would.

He cleared his throat. "That day," he said, continuing with the past, "I noticed a particular student straggling behind a large group. Tall, slender, a bit gangly with curly blond hair streaked with platinum."

Delilah squirmed uncomfortably.

"He was the spitting image of one of my oldest friends, the Viscount Archer. But for one not-insignificant fact."

Delilah shook her head. "Impossible. I was perfect in that role."

"The student was Archie from fifteen or so years ago."

Delilah rolled her eyes.

"I asked the headmaster who the boy was."

"And he told you the boy was a Windermere cousin from India," she continued for him. Of course, she knew that. She'd been the one to put forward the falsehood in the first place.

He nodded. "I knew it instantly for a lie."

She heaved a frustrated sigh. "Because, as a close friend of the family, you happened to be in a position to know there are no Windermere cousins in India."

"I knew the boy for not a cousin, but a sister."

A wry laugh escaped Delilah. "And not Amelia, of course."

"*You.* Delilah. The daring sister."

The sister he couldn't seem to keep his eyes off when they were in a room together.

He would keep that last bit to himself.

"So, I asked the headmaster where that group of students was going, and he happily informed me they would be debuting a play that very night and were presently on their way to the theater for practice, which happened to be the building we were to tour. It was a stroke of luck when a teacher claimed the headmaster's attention. I wandered off on my own, hoping to get an idea of what you were up to."

"To confront me," she said, certain, the old hard glint returned to her eye.

Sebastian shook his head. "I'd decided it was none of my concern, but I was curious to see what jape you were up to. Backstage, I happened upon a group of students, but no Lady Delilah Windermere."

"Why couldn't you have simply left it there?" she asked, distress in her eyes, genuine pain and loss clear.

"Because I heard the students discussing someone. *You.*"

The time had arrived to tell her the full, hard truth.

"You were in danger."

Chapter Seven

DELILAH'S EYES SPARKED with disbelief. *"Danger?* At Eton College?" she scoffed, utterly dismissive. "Impossible."

Sebastian understood he was toeing a narrow ledge. He would tip over and lose her if he didn't explain himself. "One of them said, *And she has no idea.*"

Delilah's brow gathered with disappointment. "That's all?"

He'd done a much better job the thousand times he'd explained himself in his mind than he was doing in reality. "Then laughter."

That wiped some of the scorn off her face. "What sort of laughter?" she asked, suspicious.

"The mean sort."

"And you knew the *she* was me."

Sebastian nodded, feeling the course correct itself. "They knew the lordling Windermere from India was female, and I knew that you didn't know. Further, I knew one thing more."

"What's that?"

"They had a plan for you during that night's performance."

It only took a beat of time for Delilah to ask, "To expose me?"

"Aye."

"And you decided to stop them."

What next emerged from his mouth wouldn't show him in

the best light, but it was the truth, so it must be spoken. "I didn't."

Her eyes narrowed. "Why is that?"

Since he was being honest... "I thought it would serve you right."

She gasped. "You...you knave!"

Sebastian took the appellation in stride. He likely deserved it. "Archie is a good friend, but you Windermeres—generally speaking—could stand to have your flaunting of Society's conventions checked every so often. In fact..." If he was proceeding with honesty, he might as well out with it. "I decided to stay around for the performance, just to see it in person."

She let that settle into the air before saying, at last, "But it was you, Ravensworth. *You* exposed me." She wasn't relenting on the point. "If I was about to receive what was coming to me, why did *you* interfere?"

A fair question—and the one that struck to the heart of the matter. "It was what they said next." Sebastian still remembered how the blood had turned to ice in his veins. "*Now, explain again how we undress her?*"

As the words sank in, the outraged expression on Delilah's face froze, and she paled. "Pardon?"

Sebastian didn't need to repeat the words. "They decided that since you would be wearing a robe, it would be easy." He would leave it at that.

"To *undress* me?" she asked, as if for confirmation of what her ears surely couldn't be hearing.

"Yes."

"On the stage?"

"Yes."

"In front of an audience?"

"Yes."

A slow beat of time ticked by as all the facts came together in Delilah's mind. "Those scoundrels!" Her face brightened with a sudden idea. "Dorie claims to have some Romani blood. Perhaps she can be convinced to invoke a curse upon their heads and all their destined-to-be perfidious offspring."

"No need," said Sebastian. "I handled it."

Delilah went stone still. *"You...you handled it."*

"Once I decided that the only way anyone would be undressing you was over my dead body, it was easy to come up with a plan of my own."

Sudden realization flew across Delilah's face. "To expose me before they could."

"Simple and effective."

She exhaled a gusty, annoyed breath. "It didn't occur to you to inform me of the plot and let me manage it?"

He'd expected that question. "I did try to find you, Delilah."

Another realization passed behind her eyes. She really did have the most expressive face. "Ah."

"Ah?"

"I was a bit nervous about my first real performance," she began sheepishly. "So, I locked myself in the privy for three hours."

"Surely, there were other ways to achieve privacy—less odiferous ones." It had to be said.

"Not at a boys' school when you're a woman pretending to be a boy pretending to be a girl."

"I can see how that would require complex maneuvering."

"Unlike what people think, a proper jape is no simple endeavor. It requires planning and commitment. It's not for the faint of heart."

"No one could ever accuse your heart of faintness."

It was what he liked best about her, in fact.

She had nerve.

She had heart.

Her eyes filled with a new intensity. "You must've known that I would be angry with you."

"But you wouldn't be humiliated." That was the main point.

Her head canted. "Wasn't that as much as a high-flying Windermere deserves every so often?"

"You didn't deserve that."

That seemed to take the wind out of her sails as she released a breathy, "Oh."

He could stop here—he *should* stop here—but truths that wanted out had been too long pent up. "You possess a wildness, Delilah."

She snorted. "All England, Scotland, and possibly Wales know that."

"I have no desire to see it tamed."

Her mouth snapped shut as a flood of emotions swept across her face.

"I like knowing it's out in the world," he continued.

"I had no idea."

"You on that stage..." He couldn't seem to stop revealing truths. "It was the most foolhardy thing I've ever seen."

"That's been publicly established," she said, cool and dry as a wintry desert.

"But it was also one of the bravest."

She blinked. *"Bravest?"*

"I've never known anyone with courage like yours. When you gave that speech from *King Lear*, I understood why you'd done it."

"I had a bet with Archie that I was determined to win. And I was winning it, for the record, until very suddenly I wasn't."

Sebastian shook his head. "That wasn't why you did it. That's the excuse."

"Then tell me why I did it, since you're such an expert on me."

"Performing is your passion, Delilah. You saw an opportunity to live that passion, and you seized it." He spread his arms wide, indicating their surroundings. "Like being part of a traveling theater company. You're not doing it because you're a spoiled Windermere brat."

"Thank you?" she said with a befuddled knit of her brow.

Even as a smile wanted release, he wouldn't be distracted. "You're here because you're living your dream. I admire you, Delilah."

Even as the beat of his heart accelerated, time did the opposite and slowed. The next words that wanted to fall from his mouth... Perhaps he shouldn't speak them.

For there would be no returning from where they would lead.

But he couldn't *not* speak them.

Not in the interest of truth.

"I've always admired you."

In the exhalation of a slow breath, she seemed to be releasing something more. "You truly never were my nemesis."

"Never."

And tonight, on this secluded stretch of Norfolk beach beneath a moon that wasn't quite full, he saw in her eyes that, finally, she believed him.

He wanted to reach out and pull her toward him, press his mouth to hers.

So, he didn't.

Because he knew.

What existed between him and Delilah was combustible, and one touch of his lips to hers would be all the spark needed to create a wildfire that would blaze through and consume them both whole.

But within her eyes he didn't sense caution, but rather the opposite.

Within her eyes he saw daring and wildness and...

Determination.

He wasn't sure he could hold out against a daring, wild, and determined Delilah.

And though he should, he wasn't sure he wanted to.

ONLY A TENSE sliver of air separating her shoulder from Ravensworth's, Delilah understood something true.

Everything she'd thought about this man these last few years was wrong.

Except for one thing.

He was, indeed, a frustratingly, breathtakingly arrogant man.

"After what happened, why didn't you tell me?" she demanded. "Why are you only telling me now?"

His eyebrows drew together in a dumbfounded crease. "I didn't think it would matter to you."

"*Wouldn't matter?*" Truly, this man... "What on earth can you possibly mean?"

"If it was me exposing you or a bunch of rotten lordlings."

"Why is that?"

"Because the end result was the same. Your dream was shattered."

She could hear in his voice, see in his eyes, how that idea wounded him—as a patron of the arts and, possibly, as a...friend.

"You knew that you would receive no thanks from me, and that my ire would be directed squarely at you. And yet...you protected me."

A novel feeling stole through Delilah. She wasn't the sort of lady who ever thought she needed much protecting. In fact, she didn't read romantic novels for that very reason. But the fact was she'd been a lady very much in need of protection—and this man had given it to her with no expectation of receiving the slightest measure of gratitude.

She knew what she needed to say next. "Thank you."

"You don't have to thank me, Delilah."

"Yes, I do."

She'd been protected by this man, and she felt protected now. She'd always viewed a man's protection as a gilded cage—both alluring and costly, the price too high. But with this man, it gave her a different feeling. A feeling of security that somehow coexisted with her need for freedom. Strange and unexpected, that.

And she knew.

She had to have him.

Not to show her gratitude, like what happened between the lines of some of the racier novels that Juliet read on the sly. But simply because the pull of their magnets had become too forceful to ignore.

Her body absolutely *needed* to be touching his this very instant.

On a sudden wave of determination, she planted her palms square on his chest, using her momentum to shove him back and pin him to the ground. She grabbed his wrists and held them above his head, her face inches from his, her legs straddling his waist—the feel of him, *right*.

She knew him to be a solid, substantive man. But the substance of him now was so very real and immediate.

His golden gaze took her in evenly, even as his mouth curved into a knowing, arrogant smile.

A smile that once infuriated her.

A smile that now sparked lightning through her.

The presence of that smile told her all she needed to know—she sensed it with a womanly intuition she'd only discovered in the last few days.

She would get what she wanted from him tonight.

"What you did a few days ago," she said into the intimate space between their mouths.

"Yes?" rasped against his throat.

"Could you do it again?"

"I could."

She could hear a *but* in there. *Denial.* The man would deny her.

No.

He wouldn't.

He couldn't.

"The way I see it." A change of tack was necessary.

"Yes?"

"You owe me a debt."

A heavy beat of time passed as his gaze remained steady on hers, daring her to look away, to take back what she'd said. "That's rather cheap of you, Delilah."

"I'm not sure I care."

"You might regret it on the morrow."

She shook her head. "I regret nothing from this morning."

He was waiting for her to say more.

"Nor do I regret what happened beneath the stage."

She watched her words land on him and sink in. Until now, there had been a distance in his eyes, as if he wouldn't let him himself fully believe what she was asking of him. Now, that distance faded, and in its place expanded belief and intensity.

"*This* won't be *that*, Delilah. It will be *more*."

A shiver traced through her, lighting up every nerve ending in its path, settling deep in her center where it became a heavy throb of carnal need. She was nearly breathless with it. "Is that a promise?"

"You're being incorrigible."

"I thought you admired my passion."

"You're twisting my words."

She lowered over him until her mouth touched his ear. "Good," she whispered. "I shall twist and twist until I've squeezed what I want from them."

"And what is that?"

"*You.*"

Chapter Eight

A ND DELILAH, AT last, noticed.
It wasn't simply his solid form that she was straddling.
It was his solid length beneath her...his manhood...*him*.
The something *more* he would give her.

It struck her like a bolt *this* was what she'd been so empty for. She'd needed *this* to fill her. Instinctively, she moved her hips and ground against his hard, thick shaft.

His intense golden gaze half-lidded, a groan rumbled deep through his chest.

His responding lust sent a feeling rippling through her. It wasn't only her lust she wanted to sate; she wanted to sate his, too.

"Oh, Sebastian, I need you inside me."

"This'll be a deal more pleasurable if you consent to release my hands."

Her grip relented, and he reached up and took her face in his hands, his skin deliciously warm against the cool of her cheeks. "You are so beautiful, Delilah," he said into the space between their mouths.

She didn't make a face or try to avoid the compliment the way she usually did. It wasn't that she didn't have a concept of her beauty—she did. Her sort of beauty was quite popular in the

annals of Western art—but she always took the compliment for
what it was. A man's calculation to see how far he could get with
her.

With Ravensworth, it wasn't so.

Such words from him were worth more than the breath they
were spoken upon.

"*You* are beautiful, Sebastian," fell from her mouth.

His lips twitched, but he didn't smile. Likely, he'd never been
on the receiving end of that particular compliment. Still, he took
her words in and appreciated them as she had his. His long,
masculine fingers twined through her curls. "I like your hair."

"Isn't it too short?" Everyone said so.

He shook his head. "It's perfect for you."

That was, everyone said so—except Sebastian.

Unable to take any more, she inelegantly pitched forward and
planted her mouth on his. Well, one thing was certain. He was
certainly better at kissing than she.

This time, the smile did reach his lips. She felt it against her
mouth. She would be mortified if she didn't want him so badly.

She planted her palms to either side of his head and began to
push away, and possibly apologize, and then likely beg him to
give her another chance. But his hands tightened on her back, and
he gave her no room to wriggle away. "You're alright, Delilah,"
he said. "I'm not going anywhere."

His hold on her shifted—one hand cupping the back of her
head, the other sliding down her back over the curve of her waist
until it rounded over her bottom and squeezed, grinding her
against his rigid length. She groaned, and he caught it in his
mouth as his lips softened and took control, the tip of his tongue
sliding across her bottom lip, that slippery glide shooting a feeling
of raw want straight through her.

From the outside, kisses had always appeared chaste to her.
But Sebastian's kiss was showing her a whole new side of what a
kiss could be.

She'd never known a kiss was a carnal act.

Again, she squirmed against him. This time, they both groaned in pleasure—and frustration.

It was achingly clear there was a problem.

Too many layers of clothes stood between them.

Of course, one layer would be one too many.

Through brute strength of will, she tore her mouth from his. "Sebastian, this won't do."

His brow crinkled with bemusement. But it was action rather than words that would get her what she wanted.

She bolted upright, still straddling him. He shifted forward, propped on his elbows, eyes intent, very clearly wondering what her next move would be.

Well, she wouldn't hold him—or herself—in suspense longer than absolutely necessary. She grabbed her shirt and the chemise beneath, untucked the articles of clothing from her waistband with a few efficient movements, and flung them over her head and away.

Beneath her, he froze, taking in her brazenness and nudity. Her nipples tightened against the breeze lifting off the water and beneath the intensity of his gaze. The look in his eyes told her they were firmly—*decidedly*—on the path to *more*.

He liked what he saw.

His eyes told her that, too.

Well then, wouldn't he like to see a little more?

On sudden decision, she pushed entirely off him and sprang to her feet.

And silent, he watched.

Oh, the appreciation in his eyes. How she warmed to it.

She felt like she was on stage.

For this audience of one.

The only audience that mattered.

And though it was performance, there was no falsity to it.

She was following her instinct—and something else, too.

Something she'd never considered in the same breath that she'd ever considered this man.

She was following her heart.

)⚹

SEBASTIAN WASN'T THE sort of man who romped in haylofts.

Nor rutted against secluded tree trunks.

Nor trysted upon abandoned stretches of midnight beaches.

He simply wasn't that sort of man.

His bedsport took place upon firm mattresses clad in cotton sheets—or on the odd chaise longue in a pinch.

And yet…

Here he was, gone midnight, stretched out on a beach on the verge of tupping a woman outdoors.

And not just any woman.

Delilah.

For her, he was that sort of man.

Beneath pale moonlight and stars that winked their faraway brilliance, she stood before him, golden hair curled against her elegant neck, her breasts bare, taut, and proud. They were the most perfectly formed breasts he'd ever beheld. Breasts didn't need to be large to be perfect. So many men never understood that.

She bit her bottom lip between her teeth, and her fingers found the waistband of her skirt and tugged, loosening a button, then another. The garment fell to the sand on a muted shush, leaving Delilah as naked as Venus on her half shell.

His cock had been full before now.

Now it was adamantine.

"Come closer," he found himself saying, willing himself to remain sprawled on the ground.

It was all he could do not to ravish her here and now—for Delilah looked in need of a thorough ravishing.

And he was just the man to give it to her.

The only man.

She lowered to her knees beside him. Her gaze steady, unflinching, she said, "Now it's your turn."

He didn't need to be told twice. Over his head went his shirt, and the boots were kicked off his feet. He reached for the fall of his trousers, and her hand covered his, stopping him. "And it's my turn again," she said, mischief and intention in her eyes.

Again, he leaned back onto his elbows. Her tongue darted out to swipe across her bottom lip as her gaze roved over him. Shoulders...chest...stomach... She liked what she saw.

But he'd known that.

She had to have what she saw.

That was new.

Her gaze landed on the long, thick outline of his cock, and it throbbed—*hard*—in response. He'd long suspected Lady Delilah Windermere would be the death of him, but it was only now that possibility became certainty.

If she didn't touch him soon, he would surely turn to dust.

Fingers that trembled slipped one button from its loop. Then another, and another. Anticipation and lust built inside Sebastian to the breaking point. What sort of idea was it to allow a virgin to take the lead in a seduction, anyway?

His cock—free, *finally*—lay across his stomach, exposed, hard, and ready. She feathered her fingers across its long length. He sucked in a sharp breath.

A little smile tipped one corner of her mouth. "That couldn't have hurt."

A dry laugh escaped him. *Virgins.* He'd never been with one, and he was coming to find that one was enough. "Delilah," he said, her name a raw scrape against his throat. "What you're going to do now is wrap your hand around my shaft." Warm fingers closed around him. "And stroke along its length."

"Like this?" She squeezed tighter and tugged.

Bright sensation sparked through Sebastian, pulling all his muscles taut, sending lightning through his veins, pinpricking his skin with a light sheen of sweat. He reached out. He had to touch her. This passivity didn't suit him. "Delilah, you know what to do."

She took his meaning and held on to him even as she moved to straddle him again, her quim, wet and swollen with need, hovering above him. He grabbed hold of her waist to steady her as she slid the crown of his cock along her—oh, yes, *wet*—slit and he pressed at the opening of her sex.

He growled. An actual growl. Like an animal.

Who was this man he was becoming?

She planted her other palm on his shoulder and began to lower onto him. Inch by slow inch, she took him into her sex— her flesh swollen and tight around him—her half lidded gaze gone hazy with need. To be inside Delilah...

How long had he wanted this?

How many nights had it stolen into his dreams?

"Oh, Sebastian," she gasped. "How...*oh*...how much more of you can there be?"

"You can take it, Delilah. You can take all of me."

She went still, and a slow beat of time ticked by. "Can I?"

Quick on the question's heels, the certainty crashed in that they weren't simply talking about this carnal act. They were speaking of something less tangible—something they would need to talk about later.

For now, the carnal had its demands.

Having taken most of him in, she slowed, adjusting to the feel of him—her body bathed in moonlight...knees digging into the sand...her nipples puckered and begging for a lick...her sex, wet and effulgent, impaled on him...

How had he captured this goddess and made her his for the night?

His.

Careful, a voice warned. It would be too easy to feel like a god himself for having accomplished the feat.

Hubris.

Hubris he hadn't truly earned for he hadn't given her what she wanted.

Yet.

Toward that end, he pushed himself upright, bringing their chests to touch, their mouths so close their breath mingled. Her taut nipples pressed into him, and his hands found the hollow of her spine and the bead of perspiration trickling down, before tightening around her hips and moving her on him.

"Oh," she groaned, wrapping her arms around his neck, her loose curls tickling his cheek as she pressed her lips to his, breathing a long moan into his mouth as she began to take control of her movement, slowly, testingly, taking him in deeply, fully, not shying away from the boundaries of pleasure and pain.

This Delilah...the one entirely abandoned to herself...he'd sensed her all this time, for it was *she* who called to the *him* he kept hidden away.

The *him* who wanted and craved and ached.

For *her.*

"You're ready, Delilah."

"*Ready?*" She muttered into his neck. "For what?"

"For *this.*"

His grip tightened on her hips, and he thrust. She gasped and cried out.

"Too much?"

She shook her head. "Do it again."

He held her fast against him, grinding her on him, and thrust again. Her grip on his shoulders tightened, nails digging into flesh, and her hips joined his rhythm, carrying her toward the place she sought. He saw it in the determined intensity of her movements, the crease of her brow, the concentration of purpose. Release was beginning to taunt her, just out of reach.

Too soon, came a protest.

He wasn't ready for her to be finished with him.

And yet the pull to give this woman what she wanted was too strong. He began moving her up and down his shaft, her quim a delicious tight slide on him, and again she cried out. "Sebastian...you're so much."

She was close as she strained and strived for release. And then she went tense and still, caught in the grasp of the moment before release—the uncertain instant it could go either way—before breaking, her sex pulsing around his length, entreating him to tumble over the edge with her.

And then it was upon him—the taunt...the tease...the demand that he give over—and he was pumping his climax into Delilah, joining her in the realm he'd experienced countless times, with countless partners, but never with her.

And never like this.

His arms tightened around her, and she slumped against him, enervated, her heart matching his beat for beat, her breath ragged against his neck.

"That was," she spoke against his skin.

The remainder of the sentence hung in the air and drifted away on the breeze.

It didn't need to be spoken anyway. Words were highly overrated. People tended to waste far too many of them when a meaningful silence was sufficient.

Seconds and minutes beat by, and their bodies remained entwined, until at last—*too soon*—movement became necessary. She lifted her head, her eyes questioning. She was wondering about him, about this man she'd thought she'd known for years, but tonight had revealed himself to be a different man.

Nay, not different, but *more*.

And she would be wondering about herself.

About what she'd just done with that man.

"Delilah, can we talk?"

He was finding himself in need of some words to be spoken between them.

"Perhaps," she said before pushing back, and off him. The loss of her stole through him cell by cell, leaving a trail of emptiness in its wake.

"That was—" She searched for a word. "*Amazing.*"

A laugh startled out of him. It couldn't help itself. "You're not supposed to say things like that after a tup."

"Why not?"

"Because..." And he couldn't think of how to finish the sentence, but not because he didn't understand *why not*.

It had to do with the games borne of power and distrust that lovers played. Games he didn't want to play with Delilah. He'd never been interested in games, anyway, even as a child.

But in those times he did play, he played to win.

"Come with me," she said, her slender hand slipping into his.

"Where?" he asked, the question a reflex. The truth was he'd go anywhere with her.

But he wasn't ready to speak that truth aloud.

Yet.

And who was he trying to fool with that nonsense that he didn't play games?

She jutted her chin toward the ocean, mischief in her eyes.

"You go ahead," he said.

A quick smile tripped across her mouth, and she slid her hand from his before springing up and running straight into the ocean, splashy laughter trailing in her wake.

He pushed off the sand and followed, unable not to. "Come somewhere with me tomorrow," he called out.

"The company is decamping tomorrow."

Blast.

A playful splash of water landed on the side of his face. He sputtered salt water from his mouth. "Delilah, be careful of the consequences of your actions," he said, wading toward her through waves that now reached his waist.

"I am," she said, now floating on her back. "*Always.* But here's the thing, Sebastian. I generally find my provocations to be worth the consequences."

She directed another well-aimed spray of water at him.

Head averted, he braved the sloshy onslaught until he came close enough to gather a giggly Delilah into his arms, their naked bodies slick against each other. "Come somewhere with me when we make camp again," he entreated. His mouth found her neck. It couldn't help itself. His cock grew heavy.

"Anywhere," she exhaled, throwing her arms around his neck, and her legs around his waist, weightless, his hard manhood pressed against her hot cunny.

Even as he took a taut nipple into his mouth and sucked, and she reached between their bodies and guided his shaft to the entrance of her sex...even as he pressed inside her...he vowed this wasn't the only way he would have Lady Delilah Windermere.

He would make more than her body his.

Chapter Nine

A week later

S CENE REHEARSAL FINISHED for the day, Delilah's mouth watered at the prospect of the mince and potato pasty in her hand.

She took the caravan steps two at a time—a benefit of her long legs—and poked her head inside, her eyes adjusting quickly to the gray light within. Her gaze immediately found Flora and Dorie, who went instantly quiet. They'd been in conversation...about her. That was what the cut-off silence and the funny smiles they were casting in her direction said.

In an instant, she knew why, her heart beating out a few extra thuds as her gaze shifted toward her bunk.

There, arranged upon her homespun pillow, lay a single flower.

Not a rose or peony or the sort of flower that would require cultivation in a conservatory or formal garden.

A wildflower—the sort plucked directly from a field.

And this wasn't the first wildflower. Every day a different one appeared. Yesterday, it had been a pale pink milkmaid, and the day before a cheery purple columbine.

Today, it was her favorite: a simple white daisy.

She lifted the flower and held it to her nose. A light scent of grass and country air. *Lovely.*

Today, however, she noticed something new on her pillow

alongside the flower. A folded square of paper.

Beneath the watchful, knowing eyes of Flora and Dorie, she took it between forefinger and thumb, only just thinking not to bring it to her nose, too. It would smell of citrus and cedar, that much she knew.

"Got yourself a man who can read and write. That'll be a keeper," said Dorie on a broad laugh.

"And I wonder who that man might be," said Flora with a suggestive waggle of her eyebrows.

Seb.

No one needed to say it. In a theater company who spent most of their waking hours together, there were no secrets—and not much need for any, either.

Seven mornings ago, after Sebastian had walked her to the caravan and kissed her breathless at the steps, Dorie had let out a long, low whistle and Flora had giggled like a schoolgirl. And when Delilah had laid her head down on her pillow and closed her eyes, she heard, "A lass doesn't let one like Seb go."

And that had been the end of it. There was no shame. No imposing Society's rules of propriety upon her. She was allowed to *be*—and if she wanted to be with Seb, then that was her business.

Now, she opened the note.

Meet me at the village path at one o'clock.

She consulted her pocket watch. That left her fifteen minutes.

The fact was she hadn't spoken to him since that night— *morning.*

She hadn't been avoiding him, per se. It was simply that the company had been so occupied with packing up camp and moving inland, at first. Then they'd been busy making camp. Then it was on to practices, performances, and sleep.

Which wasn't to say she hadn't been keeping half an eye on him. *Seb*—a man she hardly knew.

And yet knew so well.

A man her body couldn't forget.

A man an inconvenient part of her wanted to know better.

He'd been giving her room to know her mind. She understood that. But the wildflowers on her pillow...

He'd also been letting her know she wasn't far from his.

Determination seized her, and she scarfed her pasty in five unladylike bites and swiped the crumbs from her mouth with the back of her hand. She caught a quick glance of herself in the mirror and gave her cheeks a few pinches for color. She took the daisy and tucked it behind her ear. Gentle laughter met her back as she clambered down the caravan steps.

At the edge of camp, she found him. *Seb.* Waiting.

For her.

That this handsome man with a seriousness in his eyes should be waiting for her...

It sent a thrill through her.

How attractive he was in his plain workman's clothes. Tall. Broad of shoulder. Dark blond hair streaked with summer sun. Moss-flecked, golden eyes intent upon her.

She'd never known a man's serious gaze to be an aphrodisiac.

But this man's serious gaze was.

She could ravish him here and now—the rush of desire was so strong.

He pushed off the tree he'd been propped against.

"Seb," she said, only half ironic. That Ravensworth was Seb, well, it still took a bit of getting accustomed to.

"Lilah." A smile twitched about his mouth. She wasn't the only one adjusting to this new reality of them.

Them?

How was it possible there was such a thing as *them?*

He held out his arm for her. As she twined her hand through, a shiver of warmth traced through her. Such latent, tensile strength beneath layers of shirt and coat.

They fell into quiet cadence on the path that led away from the camp. The only sounds were of crunchy footsteps, birdsong, and a light summer breeze rustling through the leaves of the canopy above.

"Have you been to the village?" he asked, the first outlying buildings coming into view.

She shook her head. "I haven't had the chance yet."

"Morgan gave you the role of Amelia, I heard," he said. "A good deal of new lines to memorize, I reckon."

"I don't mind in the least."

It was her first lead role, and her inaugural performance was tomorrow night. She wasn't about to muck it up.

"You'll knock them all dead, Lilah."

A shy smile found its way to her lips. How could it not?

"So, what do you know about Stratford-upon-Avon?" he asked, changing the subject.

She shrugged and glanced around. "A lovely, little village perched upon a river, it would appear."

Incredulous eyes met hers. "You truly don't know its significance?"

"Should I?"

A pleased, enigmatic smile tipped about his mouth. "You'll see."

The path ended on the high street, and they entered the mellow hustle and bustle of the village returning to their labors after midday tea. It truly was a lovely, slow-moving village, but nothing about it particularly stood out to Delilah. What was Sebastian on about?

He brought them to a stop before a slightly dilapidated square building done in the wattle-and-daub style of a few centuries ago. She didn't understand the self-satisfied look on his face. This building was nothing to look at. "I think you'll have to explain."

He extended an arm. "Behold, the birthplace of William Shakespeare."

It took a moment for the words to sink in before an astonished, "What?" flew from her mouth. "How is that possible?"

Sebastian shrugged. "Even extraordinary men have to be born somewhere."

"But here?" Her gaze shifted toward the man beside her—the man who had given her this gift. "*You* are an extraordinary man."

He shrugged, but didn't deny it.

He was an arrogant man, too, lest she forget.

"Shall we go inside?" he asked.

"We can?"

"I've made arrangements."

Delilah snorted. Of course, he had. Seb was still Ravensworth.

He produced a key and turned the lock. Three steps inside the empty house, Delilah sneezed. Murky, dust-riddled light poured in through mullioned windows encrusted with the grime of a hundred years. The atmosphere was close and dark, the sort produced centuries ago when plague still roamed the country and light was meager. Different times, those of Shakespeare, when life felt wobbly and precious and abbreviated. It was Shakespeare with his words and genius for entertainment who helped pull people out of those medieval years of darkness and uncertainty and into a more modern age.

And here he'd been born. Here he'd strained against leading strings and learned the letters that would become words—words that would transform literature.

Sebastian cast his gaze about. "This place has potential," he said, his voice a hollow echo.

Delilah's head whipped around to find him inspecting the wide hearth framed with soot-encrusted brick. "*Potential?*" Surely, she couldn't have heard him correctly.

"It could be altered here and there to—"

"*Altered?*" Her brow crinkled. "Why would anyone do such a thing?"

"Why not?"

A possibility occurred to her. "You cannot be thinking of buying Shakespeare's house."

"Why not?" he repeated.

Oh, the overweening privilege of this man. Knew it no

bounds?

"I forbid it," she said, firm.

"You *forbid* it?"

It did sound ludicrous when he said it like that. Who was she to forbid the Duke of Ravensworth anything?

But she'd chosen this hill to make a stand, and she would hold her position. "I do."

He laughed.

From the pit of his stomach.

Another possibility occurred to her... "No one's ever forbid you anything, have they?"

"I can't say they have." He crossed his arms over his chest and propped a shoulder against a hearth beam. "And what wouldn't you change about this house?"

"The smell," she answered without hesitation.

"The *smell?*"

"It needs to smell exactly as it does now."

"Like soured apples?"

Delilah nodded. "We are breathing the same air as Shakespeare."

A few ticks of time beat by, and he nodded. In his eyes, she saw understanding.

Was it possible that Sebastian, the Duke of Ravensworth, understood *her?*

Deep down—*improbably*—she knew the answer.

SEBASTIAN'S STEP SEVERAL paces behind Delilah, he followed as she took the lead in exploring the house.

Around the great room. Down a narrow corridor with low ceilings, close, dark, rife with whispered conversations past. Into the kitchen, stale and dank from years of disuse—a room that longed to be the warm beating heart of a household. Through the door that led into the kitchen garden overgrown with weeds and herbs alike. Delilah pinched a leaf of thyme and brought the fragrant leaf to her nose, emitting a coo of delight.

"Shakespeare's thyme," he couldn't help saying.

She smiled and tucked the leaf into her skirt pocket.

She returned to the kitchen and found the narrow, steep staircase. Up creaking rungs she climbed, him behind her, until they reached a loft, low-ceilinged and just wide enough to accommodate a few cots and perhaps a small writing desk. This would've been the children's room.

"Shakespeare would've slept here," she tossed over her shoulder.

"Likely."

She pointed. "There, beneath the dormer window."

A dry laugh sounded through Sebastian's nose. "And how would you know that?"

"Because that's where Juliet would sleep. Dreamers and writers are in constant need of windows to stare out of." She glanced at him, and a laugh chirruped out of her. "You're entirely too massive a man for this loft."

It was true. His forehead had struck two support beams already. "Shall we make our descent?"

On the ground floor, Delilah inhaled another sip of Shakespeare's air before following Sebastian through the front door and out of the house. "That was wonderful," she said as they fell into step on the high street.

"Then I take it you're a believer," said Sebastian.

"A believer?"

"In Shakespeare."

"As...*what?*...a diety?"

He shook his head on a laugh. Oh, the things Delilah said. "As a writer."

"You'll have to explain."

"There are rumblings that Shakespeare as we know him is a fraud."

"How so?"

"That he was an actor and man of business who took credit for others' words." He spread his hands wide. "Or that time has given him credit due others without anyone's say-so."

"And the reasoning behind these theories?"

Sebastian shrugged. "Two things. The sheer quantity of the work found in the folios published after his death. There is simply so much of it, and he didn't live to be all that aged. As an actor and man of business, where would he have found the time?"

Delilah appeared entirely unmoved. "And the other theory?"

"He was lowborn. Some feel that only a gentleman could've written those lines."

Delilah snorted. "Shakespeare can't win, can he?"

"How so?" asked Sebastian, interested in her perspective.

"Either multiple men wrote the works attributed to him, or if a single man did, it could've only been a highborn, Eton-educated aristocrat."

"A Harrovian might be an acceptable possibility," he said, dry.

She cut him a curious glance. "What do you think?"

Sebastian allowed a few footsteps to fall behind them while he gathered his thoughts. "It's in the expression of the deepest, darkest motivators of humanity that we find the heart of Shakespeare," he said. "And I've yet to meet a highborn, Eton- or Harrow-educated aristocratic male capable of expressing humanity's deepest, darkest motivators beyond belly or cock."

A delighted laugh escaped Delilah. "Yourself included?"

"Possibly."

Her smile remained wide even as her eyes narrowed. "So, *you*—a *duke*—believe a lowborn man to have been one of the greatest writers in history?"

Sebastian nodded. "I do. As a patron to many sorts of artists, I've observed those gifted by the muse at close quarters, and I happen to know she doesn't give a sod about one's birthright. She strikes and gifts where she wills."

Delilah cast a surprised glance his way. "How very poetic,

Your Grace. Have you been struck by a fever?"

"Erm, no."

"I've never heard you speak so."

And she liked it.

That was what he heard in her voice. Still... "To be fair, Delilah, we hardly conversed before a few weeks ago."

She nodded pensively. "Our conversings were conducted more in the mode of guerilla skirmishes."

A dry laugh sounded through his nose. She wasn't wrong.

They reached the River Avon—and the punt for two tied to the small dock exactly where he'd instructed. "After you, milady," he said, his hand extended to assist her into the boat.

"What is this?" she asked, even as she took his hand and placed her feet gingerly onto the bottom boards. "Another surprise? For me?"

For you, he didn't confirm. He found himself giving a non-committal grunt—he'd become quite adept at those—and stepping into the punt, untying the ropes and taking oars in hand.

He'd been rowing them down the river five or so minutes when Delilah said, "This is a decidedly aristocratic pursuit for lowly Seb the carpenter."

"I won't tell if you won't."

A smile twitched about her mouth. She truly was lovely, relaxed and reclined onto her elbows and allowing the soft river breeze to riffle through her curls. "Archie has rubbed off on you over the years, I'm afraid."

He didn't deny it. "Let's hope I've rubbed off a little on him, too."

Sebastian loved Archie like a brother, but it was only one day in ten that his friend's feet touched earth. It was a well thing he'd found the more earthbound Valentina.

"Where are we going, anyway?" asked Delilah.

"There's a place I want to show you."

"Along the Avon?"

He nodded.

"How very mysterious." She held up a hand. "Don't tell me."
A beat. "You have land here."

"As it happens, I do. Wimberley Hill."

She shook her head. "I thought you weren't a duke for the rest of the summer."

"No one will know we're there."

Intrigue shone in Delilah's eyes. *Good.* He liked keeping her on her toes.

"In Shakespeare's house—" he began.

"I still can't believe we were inside the Bard's house—breathing his air—only an hour ago."

"You mentioned Juliet," he continued. "You miss her."

Delilah nodded as if a knot had suddenly formed in her throat. "After she ran off with Rory, I saw the future stretching out without her, and it was dead lonely."

She looked surprised at herself for having spoken the words aloud, particularly the last one which emerged on a rasp. *Lonely.*

She'd been lonely. So, she'd taken her future in hand and joined the Albion Players. He admired that in her. She hadn't taken loneliness lying down.

"Juliet is like my twin," she continued. "Part of me. You know..." Hesitation hung about her. "When you discovered me with the Players..."

"Yes?"

"I wasn't happy about it."

"I seem to have a vague recollection," he said only half ironically.

"At first."

Sebastian waited.

"But now, well, I'm glad you claimed your dukely prerogative to do as you will and stayed with the company."

Sebastian allowed her words to settle into the air between them, where they nested and made themselves comfortable.

"You know, Delilah, I'm not alone in exercising my aristocratic prerogative."

"Oh?" she asked, all wide-eyed innocence, except for the self-deprecating glint in her eyes.

"I can't imagine there's anything you've wanted to do that you haven't done."

She screwed her eyes up to the sky, face scrunched, as if she were thinking hard. "I haven't attended a masquerade ball, and I've always wanted to do that."

After a few rows of the oars, Sebastian found himself asking, "Shall I throw a masquerade ball?"

"It doesn't exactly seem like your style," she said, blithely reaching out and allowing her fingertips to graze along the surface of the water.

Was she saying he was an old fogey? "I might throw one," he protested.

"And why would you do that?" Her eyes had drifted closed with the smooth glide of the punt.

"Because you would like it."

Her eyes slitted open and met his. "You would throw a masquerade ball for me?"

He held her gaze and said, "If I ever do, you'll know why."

His words didn't drift lightly away with the river breeze, but instead remained, solid, as if composed of dense substance. Delilah's head canted as she chewed on them. At last, she said, "You're a sweet man."

She spoke the words with such utter and complete surprise, a laugh almost burst from him. "Pardon?" He would give her the opportunity to take them back.

"You heard me."

He met challenge in her eyes. Rather than folding, she was doubling down.

"I'm most definitely not *sweet*."

Men simply weren't *sweet*. That was the role of women.

"You are," Delilah returned without heat. As if it were established fact, and she was simply the messenger.

"I'm not."

Her eyes narrowed. "Am I the only one who knows that about you?"

Nonplussed, Sebastian took refuge in a grunt. Anyway, they'd been punting alongside his land for the last ten minutes and the dock was now in view, which gave him the excuse to make ready for disembarkation. Then he was securing the boat and taking Delilah's hand to assist her onto dry land.

"Come with me," he said.

And she allowed her hand to remain within his.

Chapter Ten

SEBASTIAN LED DELILAH across the manicured meadows and paths of Wimberley Hill, her hand nestled within his, anticipation roaring through him.

He had a place to show her.

A place she would love.

"This might be the prettiest estate in all England," she said, her gaze casting about, enchantment curving her mouth.

"Aye," agreed Sebastian.

From its willows that draped over the Avon to sectioned-off fields, not for the use of crops and cattle, but for gardens of every variety—formal, informal, herb, poison, even a hundred-year-old maze. Grass-green open fields stretched long, too, with carefully placed ha-has dug into the sides of hills manicured by sheep whose function was purely ornamental. In the distance stood the house itself: a whimsical, three-hundred-year-old structure with its multicolored and shaped bricks, Italianate decorative columns and shaped gables, arched doorways and windows, and plentiful chimneys, each decorated in a different brick pattern.

A horse and rider appeared over the short rise. *Turner*, Wimberley Hill's estate manager. The man held a hand to his forehead before releasing it into a wave of greeting the instant he recognized Sebastian, who waved back—then waved the man on. He didn't want to spoil this day with Delilah by having to be a duke.

She'd noted the exchange, but didn't comment on it. Instead, she said, "This must be your favorite estate."

"It's certainly my mother's. I was born here."

"So you spent summers here," she said.

He nodded. "Mother made sure I wasn't treated like a duke at Wimberley Hill. In London, or at the family seat, it was impossible. People naturally defer to a duke, even when he's three years old. But, here, she ensured I could be a child."

Delilah cut him an insightful glance. "For all your dukely privilege, that couldn't have been easy."

He shrugged. "Perhaps, but easier than many upbringings." It had to be said. His association with the arts world had brought him into contact with people who faced genuine struggle in their lives. His was nothing to it.

Delilah took his meaning. "Sometimes, I forget how lucky I am to have my family, for all their quirks."

He led her up the short rise of a hill, and his heart kicked into a gallop. The place he wanted to show her was just on the other side.

Once they topped the rise, Delilah came to a sudden stop at the sight spread below them. "What is this?" she murmured.

"I think you of all people would know."

Her gaze, full of awe and befuddlement, swung to meet his. "But a Roman amphitheater..." she trailed and began moving again, down the slope of the rows arranged in a semicircle of seating, toward the stage at the base. She would want to stand on that stage and test its feel and sound. She wouldn't be able not to.

He followed, slowly, allowing her the space to explore.

She met his gaze over her shoulder. "Why would you build this?"

He shrugged. "A whim."

She reached the stage and pushed herself up onto its stone surface. She stared down at him, making him the recipient of the entirety of her attention. "You're not a whimsical man."

The true reason—the one he'd kept suppressed all this time—came to him.

For you.

Two simple words he couldn't speak.

Not yet.

As Delilah prowled the stage from one end to the other, weaving in and out of columns constructed in the Greek Doric style, Sebastian joined her. "The idea had been floating around in my mind for a while." His mother and Turner thought he was becoming an eccentric when he'd shared the construction plans. He'd shrugged off their lifted eyebrows and done as he'd pleased, as ever exercising a duke's imperative. "This estate doesn't produce much by way of crops or cattle," he explained. "It's mostly ornamental."

"So, you figured why not construct a Roman amphitheater?" She canted her head in curiosity. "To what end?"

Ah, she'd struck at the heart of the matter—what he hadn't yet told anyone. "I have an idea for the amphitheater—and the entire estate, actually."

She propped her shoulder against a column. "Which is?"

"A place for artists."

"Pardon?"

"Where they could stay for intervals and do nothing but create."

A beat of time passed. She was assessing him. Not his person, but *him.* "I've never heard of such a place." She snorted and shook her head. "So, you truly aren't involved in arts patronage for the opera singers?" Her levity faded into utter seriousness. "But, Sebastian, you're no dilettante. You're the genuine thing. Your soul is in this idea." She canted her head. "Why?"

"Early in my life—during my teen years—I saw that my social position afforded me the opportunity to support the arts. I always admired the freedom of those who could express themselves in a such a way."

"But not everyone with talent has the freedom or opportunity to create," she intuited.

"So, I thought Wimberley Hill could provide a sanctuary for those in need to create in a secure, wide-open space."

A new light entered Delilah's eyes. It looked suspiciously similar to the one when she'd called him sweet. "And you've found a place for yourself in the world of artists," she said, earnest. "You're a necessary part of it."

He shook his head. "I wouldn't take that much credit for myself, but I do have the privilege of being involved in shaping that world and ensuring it continues on."

She blinked as if seeing him for the first time.

And perhaps she was, for this was the first time he'd truly bared his soul to her.

"You're on a mission, aren't you?"

"Art shows a nation its soul," he said. "And it allows a nation to express its soul. It matters as much as or more than military might. It shows us who we are and lights the way toward who we could be. It's all there in the notes of an aria or the brushstrokes across a canvas or a line from the Bard. Art is intrinsic to our humanity."

And he'd laid himself bare to Delilah.

It felt terrifying and good and *right*.

She walked to the end of the stage and sat, her legs swinging over the edge, as she faced the rise of empty seats. "I think it's my turn to tell you something about myself."

Sebastian understood her words as an invitation. To sit beside her. To know more of her than she'd yet revealed.

"I need to tell you what led to me being on stage that day."

He didn't need to ask what stage or which day. *Eton*. Still, he knew something of the details. "You and Archie had a bet, correct?"

"It did start that way," she said, tentative. "Archie wanted to pull one over on Eton College, and as usual, I was the adoring, competitive baby sister seeking the approval of her older brother. We decided my stint at Eton as a Windermere cousin would last the length of the short summer term."

"And Archie bet you wouldn't succeed in the role."

She nodded. "But here's the thing. I did succeed. I was admitted and began attending classes as a shy little lordling."

"A coup, to be sure."

A dry laugh escaped her. "It was utterly exhilarating." Then she exhaled a sigh. "It would've and should've succeeded, and I would've and should've won the bet without causing my family a load of scandal, but I made one crucial mistake."

"Which was?"

She shook her head as if she herself couldn't quite believe her past actions. "I signed up for the term-end play."

And Sebastian understood. "Hubris."

"We Windermeres are in no short supply," she conceded. "I was so absolutely heady with having succeeded in my impersonation of a lad of thirteen years that the play seemed a natural extension of my role. I was the sort of lad who would act in the end-of-term play."

Sebastian sensed a *but*.

"*But* that was simply a lie I told myself." She let that truth sink in for a few seconds. "The play was too much of a temptation—my one opportunity to perform on stage in front of an audience. Not an audience of family and friends, as I'd done since I could toddle about without falling over. An audience of strangers. People who could judge my work honestly. Any smiles and laughs would be genuine—any tears, too. This was what I'd been craving since I first realized the stage was my passion."

"And an opportunity you might never have again."

"I'm a lady, born and bred, and ladies don't take to the stage."

"Except as a novelty."

"And I couldn't reduce myself to that. I do have my pride." She squared her shoulders, as if reliving the day. "I decided this was it."

"And you came close."

"So close," she said, wistful. "Until you ruined everything."

Though they sat nearly shoulder to shoulder, Sebastian felt an unbridgeable chasm open between them. "Delilah—"

Her crystalline azure eyes met his, stopping unformed words in his mouth. "And saved me."

And like that, the space between them collapsed, as if the elements of his and her bodies had dissolved—any barriers between them gone.

He needed to touch her.

He needed to make her his.

IT WAS IN the black flare of his pupils that Delilah first intuited the shift in Sebastian's intention.

She'd come to understand a few things about this man.

He knew what he wanted.

And he took what he wanted.

And in the taking, he gave.

A shiver of anticipation whizzed through her.

"Delilah, what do you want?"

"What?" she asked, filled with sudden nerves. She knew what he was asking. She also knew she wouldn't get what she wanted if she played coy. She took a bracing sip of air and leapt. "To be utterly ravished."

His eyes searched hers and must've found what he was looking for. "Who am I to deny a lady what she wants?" he spoke low, reaching out to cradle the back of her head, to pull her closer.

It was the look in his golden gaze. It had shifted into the dark and determined, the unknowable, yet...*not*.

Her body knew it.

Desire.

And she knew something more: why the ladies of the *ton* practically swooned when the Duke of Ravensworth so much as entered a room. It wasn't as simple as his dashing good looks and title. It was that something else in his gaze—the dark and determined...the unknowable. Women who had experienced something of life—something of men—went wild for Ravensworth.

And in this moment Delilah understood why.

In this moment she'd become one of them.

A woman absolutely mad for the Duke of Ravensworth.

He tugged her close, his breath now grazing across her mouth. Her lips parted, and her eyelashes brushed the tops of her cheekbones in anticipation of that first touch. Just as their lips met, she breathed a sigh into his mouth. His tongue darted inside and immediately deepened the kiss, his other hand sliding around her waist and pulling her forward so it wasn't only their lips that met, but their bodies, too.

This was no tentative kiss.

This kiss knew where it was going.

And, oh, how desperate she was to follow its lead.

His mouth never left hers as he shifted, turned, and landed on his feet in a smooth motion, parting her knees with one hand, and moving into the space between.

The faint voice of reason sounded within Delilah, and she tore her mouth from his. Cheeks flushed, panting, they stared at one another. The dark intention in his eyes hadn't abated one bit. "Won't we be seen?" She had to ask.

He looked utterly nonplussed. "Of course not."

"But servants," she protested, weakly. Her heart wasn't invested in this protest. Still… "Your estate manager knows we're here."

"Precisely."

"*Precisely?*"

"They know to stay away."

"How can you be sure they will listen?"

A sardonic glint shone in his eyes. "Because I am Ravensworth."

Seb was gone. Here—between her trembly legs, in fact—stood Ravensworth.

Direct and certain...

Entirely too arrogant...

Entirely too attractive.

Oh, how she desired this man—with all his dark intention and arrogance.

He angled his head and pressed his mouth to the space just behind her ear as he began bunching up her skirts.

"Don't you want to make love on a stage?" he spoke against her skin.

The breath stuck in her lungs. The very idea... It felt so...*transgressive*. And yet... "Yes," she near whimpered.

He angled back, the knowing glint in his eyes sending a streak of lust straight through her. He brought his thumb to his mouth and gave it a long, slow lick. Then he reached between their bodies, between her parted legs, and stroked the slick finger along her slit, all the while watching her reaction. "You like that, don't you?"

"Oh, yes."

He sank to the ground, so he now knelt before her as if she were his goddess and he naught more than a supplicant. He slid her skirts further up her thighs, coarse fustian sliding across her skin. Anticipation fizzed through her, slipping molten through her veins, sending goosebumps racing across her skin.

Wider, he pushed her knees apart. A cool wisp of air brushed across her exposed quim. His irises became thin golden rings as his gaze lowered to the brazen, bare sight of her, sending a bolt of heat through her—the give and take of desire...the way that give and take only enhanced it. "Delilah, the sight of you..." His gaze flicked up to meet hers. "Shall I describe *you* to you?"

Oh, my.

She nodded.

"Pink," he said and kissed her inner thigh, "and glistening"— another kiss...higher...*closer*—"and effulgent like a hothouse flower in bloom."

Alongside lust and pleasure traced another feeling. One she

couldn't examine in this moment, but one that might keep her up nights in the future.

"Remember what I did with my fingers under the stage?"

"How could I forget?"

Truly.

"There's another way." Oh, the wickedness that shimmered off him. "It feels even better."

Chapter Eleven

B EFORE DELILAH COULD ask how that could possibly be true,
Sebastian's mouth continued its trail up the sensitive skin of
her inner thigh, and a held sigh poured out of her. "That
feels...*oh*..."

The rest of the sentence became lost to history as his mouth
moved along her thigh, his tongue a wet slide up...up...up... Her
sex throbbed... It ached... It needed... It *demanded.*

Could it be that where his fingers once touched her his
mouth would—

Oh.

Slick and warm his tongue stroked her slit. "Sebastian," she
moaned.

He chuckled against her. As his tongue flicked, his thumb
entered her, sliding in and out as he took control of her body—of
her wants and desires.

As he took control of her pleasure.

Her booted heels pressed against his shoulders, she leaned
back onto her elbows and let him touch her and fill her, deliver
pleasure to her with each flick of his tongue. Oh, the sight of
him—the feel of him—between her legs... In literature and in life,
women were always portrayed as the more sensual of the sexes.
But gazing upon this man, his eyes holding hers, daring her to

look away as he pleasured her with his tongue, she knew it to be a fundamental untruth.

This man was pure sensuality.

Impossible that she'd never seen what others so clearly saw.

This man with his unknowable gaze...his wicked smile...his unapologetic arrogance...was sin personified.

Tempting her into sin with him.

She'd never been all that adept at resisting temptation.

A Windermere trait, truth told.

Another finger entered her and she lost all capacity for thought as her body became a vessel for the pleasure he delivered. Sensation built beneath his talented tongue—curled inside her sex. It was a feeling she'd come to know... Her entire being now centered in the place where the firm tip of his tongue met her most sensitive flesh...where his fingers entered her.

Then he sucked her nub into his mouth, his tongue softly brushing and teasing her...laving...stroking...a gathering of sensation occurring within her as release held itself out of reach, taunting her with promise...then all that was collapsed inward, released as if on a spring, her body filling with light and air and color as she cried out and tumbled over the edge of climax, her sex pulsing around his fingers, him watching her with that dark intensity that only increased her pleasure.

He gave her quim one final lick and lifted his head. "I'd say you liked that."

A wicked smile on his mouth, he wiped his chin with the back of his hand. It occurred to her that she should feel a modicum of shame or modesty.

She felt neither.

"I suppose this is what people are talking about when they refer to a tup," she said.

Oh, the arrogance curving his talented mouth as he rose and stepped between her legs, his fingers making quick work of his trouser buttons. Gravity took the cloth, and his cock sprang free. *Thick...turgid...ready.* Oh, the heat that blazed through Delilah as he took a thigh in each hand, and his heavy length slid along her sex, his manhood hard against her opening. "*This* is what's referred to as a tup."

And he pressed into her, one slow, intentional inch at a time. A long moan poured from her. She didn't recognize herself as he impaled her. So hard...so big...filling her with sensations only he could offer.

And didn't the expression on his face say he knew it.

And—oh, heaven help her—didn't she find it entirely too attractive.

As he began to slide in and out of her, it occurred to her that her body might be forming a dependency on this man. That when summer ended she might not be able to give him up. But— *oh*—how could she possibly when he made her feel like *this*?

Her legs wrapped around his waist, bringing him yet closer. She reached up and pulled his mouth to hers, taking this act to another level of intimacy, as she ground against him, his full, heavy length skating along the sharp straightedge between pleasure and pain.

He sucked his breath and uttered, "Delilah," with raw ache and need, the utterance rumbling through her so that she nearly climaxed again on the spot.

Of a sudden, he shifted back and out of her, provoking a cry of outrage. "What do you think you're—"

"I thought you wanted a proper tup."

And with that he tugged her forward and off the edge of the stage so her feet touched ground, immediately taking her hips in hand and turning her around. Her bottom bared to the breeze, his hand found the middle of her back and subtly pushed, leaving her no choice but to bend at the waist and plant her palms on cool stone. The hand trailed up her back and wove through her hair, her hips angled so her bottom curved up.

Over her shoulder, she met his gaze just as he pushed at the opening of her sex, entering her, his fingers clutching her hair, his other hand pressed at the small of her back as he held her steady and guided his cock in and out of her with deliberate intention. Hot sensation took wing inside her. This...*tupping*...felt a bit wrong...a bit perverse...a bit like what happened in dark alleyways and gardens in the dead of night...like what happened between the lines of the warnings given by chaperones...

And like everything *right*.

Oh, all she could do was feel as he moved in and out of her, his breath ragged and desperate at her back. An odd feeling of power surged within her. That she could make this man—the arrogant Duke of Ravensworth—desperate for her...

Oh, that was conquest.

At least in this moment.

And this moment was all that mattered as she angled her hips to receive more of him and meet him stroke for stroke, his equal in this tupping. He wasn't the only one able to deliver pleasure.

He subtly pulled her hair so she arched back. "Delilah," came his voice in her ear. "I'm almost there."

"Oh, yes," she returned, the now-familiar sensation coiling in her sex. "Faster," she demanded, meeting him stroke for stroke.

He accommodated, but not as deeply, somehow intuiting what she needed—what would get her *there...faster.*

Then release was breaking upon her, making her cry out, and behind her, both of her hips in his hands, he followed, shouting his release to the sky above.

She collapsed forward onto her elbows, and his movements, inevitably, slowed, the ragged in and out of his breath at her back. Though they'd...*tupped*...not unlike animals, she suspected—or perhaps like humans desperate for each other, came a more generous thought—she experienced connection. From her body to his, yes, but somewhere else, too.

A place that channeled deep enough to cause a dull ache inside her chest.

Was it possible that Ravensworth had connected to the place that beat faster at the merest thought of him?

It was a possibility that wasn't as troubling as she would've once supposed.

)℅

HAD HE TRULY tupped Lady Delilah Windermere like a common strumpet?

That was Sebastian's first thought as he reentered his body.

And had she truly enjoyed it?

That was his second thought.

Then he turned her around, met her thoroughly sated gaze, and knew the answers to both questions.

Yes and *yes*.

"We'll eventually make it to a proper bed," he said, striving for a note of levity.

No responding smile found its way to her swollen, kiss-crushed lips. Instead, she stared at him with uncharacteristic seriousness. "I think..." She was weighing her words. "I think I might like you."

He blinked. "You *think*? You *might*?"

Truly, Delilah... What was he going to do with her?

He reckoned he could tup her again.

She looked amenable to suggestion.

He snorted.

Actually, he knew precisely what he wanted to do with her.

But it wasn't something he could demand.

It was something he needed to ask.

And she needed to agree.

He buttoned the fall of his trousers, deciding he should be fully dressed for what he was about to say. "You seem to enjoy, erm—" He cleared his throat. He might've started all wrong. Perhaps it was a trifle inelegant to tell a lady that her sexual appetite resembled that of a wanton—though a compliment.

Delilah, however, appeared to gather where the sentence had been heading, and didn't seem the least offended. "A good tup?" There was the smile returned to her mouth.

"Erm, yes." *Oh, Lord.* "Do you know how you could have a good tup whenever you liked?"

She reached for him, hooking a finger into the waistband of his trousers and tugging him forward, a saucy glimmer in her eyes. "How's that?" She wasn't truly asking. "By making you my love slave?"

"Or," he countered, summoning his last shreds of will. Her idea wasn't a bad one. "Marriage."

The smile froze on her lips, but a saucy echo of itself.

"Haven't you ever considered it?" he asked. Most women did.

"Why should I?" She looked genuinely nonplussed. "If I shackled myself to a man, what would I receive in return? Someone who would happily accept my dowry and strip me of my freedom?"

"You don't think there's a man out there who wouldn't? A man who would respect you as an equal?"

"I've never met such a man."

The proclamation passed her lips with the certainty of repetition, as if it were a line she'd memorized that had become rote response.

He wouldn't let it slide by unchallenged.

"Haven't you?"

She blinked. Her eyebrows drew together. "Why would two people like us marry? We have wealth and status. You and I could live in sin and freedom forever."

Oh, these Windermeres. Didn't they understand anything? "To safeguard what we have."

She exhaled an annoyed sigh. "Why do men have to think like that?"

"Like what?"

"Like everything—including a woman—is a possession to be kept under lock and key."

"I'm not speaking in generalities, Delilah. I'm speaking of you and me—*us*. I don't think of you as a possession."

Realization lit across her face, and she gasped. "Are you proposing marriage to me?"

And Sebastian understood something.

He wasn't.

"Delilah, when you decide to marry me, it will be your idea."

Her mouth opened, then snapped shut. Opened again…and snapped shut again. She would be well within her rights to call him an arrogant, condescending arse.

But he wouldn't mind—for he knew he was right.

Delilah possessed a wildness to her heart that would ever demand to be free. To rush her would be the height of foolishness. Besides, summer yet held a couple of weeks in it—weeks to woo and win her.

For her to decide she would be his.

That much he knew—even if she didn't yet.

Once she'd regained her capacity for speech, she said, "I suppose we should return to camp." She pushed off the stage and smoothed her skirt. "I'll need to run my lines again this evening."

She wanted a change of subject, and he agreed it was likely for the best. They began retracing their steps across Wimberley Hill toward the docked punt. "Are you nervous about tomorrow night's performance?"

"Yes."

She moved alongside him, but didn't reach for his hand. His fingers felt empty without hers twined through. He could only hope she felt the same.

"But that's what makes it so exhilarating," she continued, her cheeks bright with passion.

The way her fervor shone through when she spoke of performance…

It gave him hope.

Lady Delilah Windermere couldn't live without her passions.

Now he could only hope he was one of them.

And he knew.

He more than liked this woman.

There was a reason he wanted to make her his—and it had

naught to do with what they'd just done on the stage.

It had to do with another feeling, one deeper and more powerful than mere desire.

But the time to tell her hadn't yet arrived.

He had another few weeks.

He had time.

Chapter Twelve

Next evening

TO SAY THE summer had gone well would be understatement. To say it ranked amongst the happiest of Sebastian's life would be hitting closer to the mark.

Even if he was presently shimmying on his belly across a beam that spanned the width of the stage fifteen feet below, toward the pulley that was causing all the trouble with the raising and lowering of backdrops. Soppitt ever gave him the least appealing tasks, and Sebastian never complained. He simply grunted his assent and set to. He'd been educated at Eton College and then Cambridge. He understood the many forms hazing took.

Although, a week ago, Soppitt had offered an explanation. "Here's the thing, Seb." He held up his calloused hand worn with decades of rough work and begin ticking off points with his fingers. "You're new. You're on the younger side. You've got muscles under them clothes. And your face is too pretty for your own good. The way I see it you need some adversity to make a proper man of you."

Sebastian responded in his usual manner. He gave a nod and a grunt and set about his task, which that day had been to dig the bog for the new camp. He would wager he was the only duke in history to dig a bog.

So, here he was, body draped over a beam, replacing a pulley wheel with about five minutes until the start of the night's performance. Task completed, he shimmied down and spotted Delilah on the other side of the stage. His first instinct was to go to her, his feet already on the move, and tell her she had this well in hand. But he stopped. She was concentrating, entering into the performance in her mind before she did for the audience.

He would leave her be—for now. He would have her all to himself, soon. The summer had taken on the glow of perfection—of them being with each other, laughing, touching, making love... She felt it, too. She must.

Only two people made for each other could experience *this*.

So, he left Delilah to her performance and made his way around the perimeter of the audience. Slouch hat pulled low, he found a three-hundred-year oak to prop a shoulder against and unobtrusively watch the panto.

From the moment she stepped on stage as Amelia in the *Lover's Vows* scene, she held the audience's rapt attention. On that stage, she contained and embodied multitudes of human experience.

Pride swelled within Sebastian. A particular sort of joy, too. She'd pursued and achieved this. And why shouldn't she have? Why was it only gentlemen who could pursue their true interests and passions? No one had ever stood in the way of him and what—or who—he'd wanted. Let them try. Why shouldn't Delilah have the same freedom?

Halfway through the scene, a voice rang out from the audience, clear as a bell, *"Lady Delilah?"*

Every muscle in Sebastian's body went suddenly tense, and on the stage, Delilah froze, all the color draining from her face. Sebastian's head whipped around, and he began scanning the audience. It was composed mostly of local families out for a night of entertainment. No one who should recognize Delilah.

"Lady Delilah Windermere, it *is* you!"

Sebastian knew that condescending, unctuous voice before his gaze, at last, landed on its owner. *Mr. Oliver Quincy.*

Sebastian didn't hesitate, springing into motion before the man could open his mouth again. As he wove through the crowd, the murmurings grew into whispers and then into open speculation as the audience began connecting the dots between the vocal gentleman amongst them and the actress frozen on stage. Perhaps they thought it part of the performance.

Perhaps this night could yet be salvaged.

Sebastian jostled his way into the row of benches where Quincy remained seated, apparently oblivious to the ruckus he was causing. His eye lit on Sebastian and brightened. "Ravensworth!"

And Sebastian realized in his rush to confront Quincy, he hadn't properly considered the consequences of that action. All eyes swung around and landed on them, eager to follow this new development.

"I hadn't the least prospect of sharing the same air as the illustrious Duke of Ravensworth when this night began!"

That well and truly put the final nail in the ruse.

The jig was up.

Quincy's eyebrows drew together in sudden befuddlement. "But why are you dressed like a...like a..."

Sebastian silently willed the man not to speak whatever nonsense that was poised on the tip of his tongue.

"Like a *peasant*."

If anything could turn a village crowd, it was that word. *Right*. Looks turned dirty and jeers grew louder as Sebastian grabbed Quincy by the arm and marched him out of harm's way. Once safely beyond reach of a potential mob situation, Sebastian released the other man, who didn't seem to comprehend the gravity of the situation.

Well, he would.

"Quincy, what are you doing here?" It had to be asked. Was no corner of England safe from this one supercilious nitwit?

Quincy tucked his thumbs into his waistcoat and rocked onto his toes. "Interestingly, a third cousin twice removed purchased an estate in the area and is having a shooting party. My invitation must've been lost in the post, but I do enjoy a day out in the marshes, so I decided to take it upon myself to accept the undelivered invitation and—"

Sebastian held up a silencing palm both imperious and pleading that Quincy immediately desist. The man looked to be settling in for a long explanation, and Sebastian hadn't the time. "What you think you saw here tonight," he said, getting straight to the main point, "you didn't see."

Quincy nodded, slowly, as if in understanding. Then he said, "What can you possibly mean? Of course, I saw what I saw. As a matter of fact, I'm seeing what I'm seeing right now. There is nothing wrong with my eyesight." He puffed out his chest. "In fact, my eyesight is quite superior to anyone's I've ever known. Which is precisely why I would be such a valuable addition to the shooting—"

Sebastian's palm lifted again. The man was indefatigable. "What you saw tonight mustn't reach the ears of London."

"Ah, but London hears all." Quincy shrugged, resigned. "Not much can be done about it."

Oh, that was where the man was wrong. "There are only three ways news of this night could reach the ears of London. Through Lady Delilah, me, or you. Lady Delilah won't be speaking of it. I sure as hell won't. Which leaves but one route."

"Oh?"

"You."

"*Me?*"

"*You.*"

Sebastian had drawn himself up to his fullest, most intimidating height, which was a good half foot taller than the man before him. He might be clothed like a "peasant"—truly Quincy's snobbery knew no bounds—but presently Sebastian was every inch the Duke of Ravensworth—with all the power and command the title conferred. A man destined to have his way. "Do you enjoy Society soirées, musicales, supper parties, balls... What have you?"

"Who doesn't?"

"Do you enjoy being a member of the *ton* who receives invitations to such gatherings?"

"Of course."

"I thought so."

Sebastian smiled, but his smile wasn't such that it invited Quincy to join in with him. Instead, the man gulped.

Still, Sebastian didn't think he'd made his point sufficiently clear. "If news of this night reaches London—*ever*—every last invitation goes away. You'll become a pariah, and you'll never receive another invitation as long as I draw breath. Is that clear enough for you?"

Quincy nodded. "'Tis," emerged like dust from the man's throat. "Your Grace," he added, ever obsequious.

Sebastian's eyes wanted to roll toward the night sky, sunk low with a thick blanket of clouds. Rain was about to break upon their heads. But he kept them trained, unflinching, upon Quincy. The other man's gaze slid away first.

Quincy taken care of, Sebastian's attention shifted toward the stage. The performance had moved on to the terrier Queen Elizabeth—she answered to Bess amongst the company—who was presently delighting the crowd.

No Delilah.

A feeling of dread sank to the pit of his stomach, as he shouldered and pushed his way to the back of the stage. Immediately, he felt the curious eyes of the theater company upon him. He chose to ignore it. Explanations could come later, but first... "Has anyone seen Lilah?" he called to anyone who would listen.

A beat of silence followed before Delilah's caravan mate Dorie stepped forward. "Is that *Lady Delilah Windermere* you're asking about?"

"*Your Grace*," finished Delilah's other caravan mate Flora.

Point made—and taken.

A few chuckles sounded around, but there was very little

amusement in it. Instead, he sensed growing distance and no small amount of distrust. Delilah would've felt it, too. Seb and Lilah were the Duke of Ravensworth and Lady Delilah Windermere—*nobs.*

His feet kicked into a sprint as he made straight for Delilah's caravan. He popped his head into the open doorway and found it empty.

And he knew.

She was gone.

And why wouldn't she be? Everything had gone disastrously and publicly wrong for her...*again.*

But this time, everything had gone wrong for him, too.

Wasn't he supposed to have had until the end of summer?

He could follow her. It wouldn't be too difficult to track her down.

But what good would that do?

Delilah needed time and space to lick her wounds. And to think... Think about what was truly lost tonight.

No, he wouldn't run after her. Not this time. This time, he would follow the advice he'd once given his good friend Rory.

Best to let a Windermere come to you.

This wasn't about him being a duke and exerting a form of power.

This was about Delilah knowing her mind—and her heart.

And following it.

Back to him.

Chapter Thirteen

Two weeks later
Casa Windermere, London

DELILAH ATTEMPTED TO concentrate on the book she was reading. She truly did. After all, *Emma* by the late Jane Austen was one of her favorite novels. This was Delilah's fifth reading of it, in fact. She'd always found it diverting.

Until this reading.

Upon this read, she found Emma Woodhouse slightly insufferable. Really a bit of a goose's bottom. It had never occurred to Delilah that a writer might dislike her heroine, but it could be that Jane Austen had disliked—even despised Emma—for it was apparent upon this reading exactly how mean-spirited and small Emma truly was.

But even more insufferable than Emma was Mr. Knightley. Delilah had always thought him dashing, but now she held a revised opinion that he was simply a dour know-it-all. Further, the blasted man was always there for Emma's worst moments—and more infuriatingly, he was always in the right.

But what Delilah truly didn't understand was why these two people wanted to marry each other!

She snapped the book shut on a tiny roar of frustration and tossed it to the other end of the settee. No matter. No one was here to see her less than civilized behavior. For two solid weeks, she'd been the lone Windermere knocking about the walls of

Casa Windermere with the servants and Valentina's cat—the aptly named Miss Hiss, who made for feral company as she occasionally gifted Delilah a mouse on her pillow. She supposed it was sweet. Still, Delilah would prefer it if the mighty huntress would allow Delilah to stroke her fur as a sign of affection. She reckoned beggars couldn't be choosers.

Delilah meandered over to the bow window overlooking the back garden still bright with late-summer blooms that had begun to fade and make way for coming autumn.

Two weeks.

It was an interminably long time to be holed up at home, waiting for inevitable scandal to follow on her heels to London. But she'd pored through all the gossip rags, daily, and there was not a whiff of it, not even in the blind items.

Sebastian had managed it.

That was what she'd come to realize.

Of course he had.

And what had she done?

Followed her first instinct.

She'd run.

She should've known she was flying too close to the sun. But the summer had been idyllic, and she'd gotten carried away in the perfection of it all—and she'd thought—*what?*—it would simply continue along that way?

As ever when she flew too close to the sun, she'd gotten scorched.

Truly, Fate had it out for her.

But that wasn't what occupied her mind.

Why was Sebastian always mixed up in her worst moments?

She darted an annoyed glare at the book laying innocently on the settee.

The man was her blasted Mr. Knightley.

But, chimed in a small voice, *isn't he also mixed up in your best moments?*

This summer... Was it perfect because she'd become a player

in the theater company? Or...

Was it perfect because Sebastian had been there, too?

She tried to swallow around the unresolved lump in her throat. It had been there these last two weeks. An interesting word—fate.

It was as if she and Sebastian were...*fated*.

And she'd run.

Like she always did.

Except this time, she'd almost immediately known it for a mistake.

And yet she hadn't turned back.

She was a person of forward momentum—and look where all that forward momentum had gotten her.

Here... Alone.

She'd followed her first instinct...

And she'd followed her worst.

Even clueless Emma Woodhouse had recognized what she had in Mr. George Knightley.

What...what had she done?

What had she lost?

She'd run...

The wrong way.

A feeling welled up inside her—the feeling that had been sitting suppressed in her stomach these last two weeks—and demanded expression. *Wretchedness.* That was the feeling—utter and complete wretchedness.

She opened her mouth, drew in a long, heavy breath, and released a loud, wet sob. One followed by another...and another...until she was a ridiculous, wailing, sodden mess.

Through her great sobs of wretchedness, however, pierced the sound of voices. Voices down the corridor that led to the receiving hall. From the chair where Miss Hiss lay curled in a tight ball, the cat's head popped up. She, too, recognized the voices. If Delilah wasn't very much mistaken, they sounded very much like...

"Delilah!" said Archie, entering the room with his usual *joie de vivre.*

"Archie," said Delilah, swiping at eyes that were surely red and swollen. Through glassy tears, she watched another figure enter the room. A small, voluptuous woman who held an elegance and reserve unique to her. "Valentina," said Delilah, rising to her feet and hugging her brother and sister-in-law in greeting. It was obvious in the cant of her head that Valentina had noted Delilah's red swollen eyes.

The instant Valentina released Delilah, Miss Hiss bounded into her true owner's arms.

"What are you doing here?" asked Delilah, a bit of accusation in her voice. But really, it was terrible timing for a social call.

Archie shrugged and settled into the chair Miss Hiss had just vacated. "This was my home the last time I checked."

Fair point.

Valentina shrugged off her pelisse. "We've only just arrived from the Continent."

Archie cocked his head at Delilah. "Wait... Aren't you in Switzerland?"

"I haven't yet mastered the trick of being two places at once." Delilah wasn't particularly in the mood for banter with her elder brother, but old habits died hard.

"Well, if you ever do, share your secret with me. I wouldn't particularly mind composing at the piano and at the same time being in my wife's—"

"*Good graces* is how I believe that sentence ends, husband," said Valentina, firm.

Mischief sparked in Archie's eyes. "If that's what you want to start calling it."

Delilah only just didn't groan. She wouldn't mind sinking into the floor at this very moment, just to escape having to witness the hot stare Archie was directing toward his wife.

More voices sounded in the corridor.

There was a God.

Into the room entered Juliet with Rory just behind. Relief soared through Delilah at the sight of her beloved cousin. Another sob hiccupped in her throat, as she rushed into Juliet's arms. "What are you doing here?"

Oh, she smelled so good and familiar.

Juliet shifted back so her direct emerald eyes bored into Delilah. How Delilah had missed this...*her.* "I received your letter."

Delilah's gaze shifted. She couldn't look Juliet in the eye and tell a flat-out lie. "It was only to inform you that I'd arrived back from Switzerland."

Juliet's gaze didn't relent. "*Early.*"

And Delilah knew that Juliet knew. Not all, of course—but enough... That something was wrong.

Delilah, who had never once dissolved into a puddle of tears in her entire life, was on the verge of doing so again for the second time tonight.

Archie finished clapping Rory on the back in greeting and turned toward Delilah. "What's all this about Switzerland, anyway?" he said. "I never had you down as one for alphorns and yodeling."

Before Delilah could slap together a decent lie, more voices sounded in the corridor. Then Amelia was striding—Amelia was a great strider, like all the Windermeres—into the room, a duchess bedecked in sumptuous ivory silk, diamonds at her wrists, throat, and even in her hair. But her splendor wasn't what made the room go silent for a beat of time.

It was Amelia's mask.

Delilah was fairly certain it had diamonds, too.

Her massive and quite handsome husband—neither fact could be ignored—Tristan entered the room behind her, wearing a simple black domino, and directed a grunt of greeting that sufficed for all the room's inhabitants. A man of few words, the Duke of Ripon.

"Amelia, Tristan," said Archie, "are you here to burgle us?"

Amelia released an exasperated sigh. Her siblings lived to

exasperate her, it was a fact. "We're on our way to the masquerade."

"*The* masquerade?" A strange premonition sparked inside Delilah.

"Who's having it on?" asked Archie.

"Ravensworth, of course," said Amelia. "His autumn equinox ball is a masquerade this year."

"Raising funds, I suppose?" asked Juliet.

"For a playhouse in Southwark, I believe," said Tristan.

At the sound of Sebastian's name, another round of wretchedness flooded through Delilah. "Why are you *here*, then?" she asked.

Her wretchedness kept compounding.

Here was Sebastian moving forward with his life.

And here she was hiding in a house.

Amelia stared at her as if she'd gone suddenly cuckoo. "To pick you up, of course."

Delilah spread her arms wide. She was wearing a simple muslin day dress—the same one she'd been wearing these last three days, truth told. She might have acquired a...*scent*. A truth that might be better left *untold*. "I had no notion of a masquerade being given by..." His name stuck in her throat. "*Him*."

"Truly, Delilah," said Amelia, "when was the last time you checked your correspondence?" She crossed the room to the correspondence desk and began riffling through the basket full of letters.

"Never," said Delilah. "Juliet is the only person who matters that writes to me, and staff know to bring those letters to me straightaway."

Juliet wrapped her arms around Delilah's waist and hugged her again. "Delilah?" she asked.

"Yes?" asked Delilah, breathing in the lovely, soul-deep familiar scent of Juliet.

"When was the last time you washed your hair?"

A fair question, and one Delilah couldn't readily answer

without the use of her fingers. It was either six or twelve days. Either way, it wasn't good. It was entirely possible she'd gone to seed.

Amelia had almost finished sorting through the correspondence. "Well, no matter. There's no invitation here, anyway."

A feeling that resembled pique sparked inside Delilah. "What do you mean there's no invitation?"

Amelia shrugged. "There isn't."

Archie rubbed his hands together. "No matter. We're all going."

"But, Delilah," said Juliet with a gleam of mischief, "Ravensworth likely wouldn't have known you'd returned early from Switzerland."

Oh, Juliet was good, Delilah would give her that. Of course, Juliet saw all. Juliet *knew*. In fact, it was possible that Juliet had known before Delilah had.

Right.

"Aha, here we have it!" Amelia exclaimed, holding up a white square of paper. "It's Ravensworth's seal." Her brow knitted for the briefest instant. "It's thicker than the one Tristan and I received."

"Perhaps it isn't an invitation at all," said Delilah, morosely. Though it was all she could do not to snatch the missive from Amelia's hand and rip it open. "Perhaps he's telling me to stay away."

All eyes landed on Delilah. If she wasn't very mistaken, the air had ripened with disbelief. "What?"

Archie snorted.

Rory shook his head with that lopsided smile of his.

Amelia simply said, "Oh, Delilah."

Tristan looked entirely uninterested in the entire business, his gaze decidedly fixed on the curve of his wife's neck.

And Juliet simply stared at Delilah…stared *into* her with those emerald witch's eyes of hers.

They all seemed to see something that she was missing entirely. Or…

Possibly…maybe she saw something, too…

"Right," said Archie, shooting to his feet. "Before we go, I must get into my wife's good graces."

"Oh?" said Amelia. "What have you done now?"

How Delilah envied Amelia's innocence.

"It isn't what I've yet done, but what I intend to do within the next five or so minutes," he said with a wicked smile.

Valentina's cheeks were twin patches of scarlet—a sure-to-be regular experience if one chose Archie for a life partner.

"What can you possibly mean by—"

Delilah held up a hand, staying the rest of the question in Amelia's mouth. "You don't want to know. Trust me."

After her siblings had finally cleared out, Delilah wandered restlessly about, eventually meandering her way to the correspondence desk when she could take the suspense no longer. She tapped her forefinger against the missive from Sebastian. It simply lay there, face up, waiting for her to open it.

Her first instinct was to resist. But…hadn't it been proven that perhaps her first instincts weren't her best?

Right.

She picked it up and tore open the seal, finding not an invitation at all, but an official-looking document. She scanned the paper, her eyes picking out one of every twenty or so words. Words like *special* and *license* and *union*.

Her hands grew slack, and the document fell onto the desk. She planted a palm onto the inlaid birch and walnut surface for support as she slid onto a chair. She lifted the paper again and began reading it closely, the words having a devil of a time sinking into her brain.

His Grace Sebastian Crewe, the Duke of Ravensworth.

That was one bundle of words.

Lady Delilah Windermere.

That was another.

Her name…united with his.

Delilah felt suddenly winded.

This wasn't a proposal of marriage.

It was more of an opportunity.

This piece of paper represented his terms if she wanted to be with him.

If, somehow, she found a way to reverse course and run...

Toward him.

"Delilah, when you decide to marry me, it will be your idea."

In the moment, she'd let the words glance off her as his usual arrogance talking. But now, they sank in and found purchase as more of his words came to her.

"If I ever do, you'll know why."

Tonight's masquerade...

It was for her.

She shot to her feet, filled with sudden determination. First, she was going to peel off this dress and toss it into the fireplace. It would never be free of her unwashed stench. Better to put it out of its misery.

Then she would give herself a good, cleansing scrub.

Then she would put on her mask—the one she'd been saving for a few years now.

She had a masquerade to attend.

And a future to claim.

She was done running away.

She was now running *toward*.

He'd better be ready.

But, first, she must wash her hair.

Chapter Fourteen

SEBASTIAN MINGLED THROUGH the crowd in his usual evening blacks. Only tonight he also wore a black silk domino.

He tried not to feel silly.

Of course, the mask didn't prevent anyone from recognizing the towering Duke of Ravensworth. Usually, the only people at any given *ton* event who could match his height were the Windermeres. But they hadn't yet arrived, which left him to the task of attentive host.

Really, he cared not if all or even a few of the Windermeres showed their—masked—faces tonight.

It was only the one who mattered.

And she wasn't here.

He knew it without looking. The chemical composition of the room would've altered if she'd entered it.

He snorted. He'd vowed to make Delilah come to him. And yet he'd thrown a masquerade ball—obviously, for her. Further, he'd sent her the special license he'd procured. He wanted her to know where he stood. But, most importantly, he wanted her to know where she stood in relation to where he stood.

There was no middle ground.

That was what she needed to understand.

Summer was beautiful, but it was a finite amount of time.

He wanted forever…

Or nothing.

The thought did nothing to improve his mood. In fact, it only plunged him deeper into foul territory.

An approaching figure caught his eye, and he inwardly groaned. *Lord Dankworth.* A name to suit the man, if there ever was one. Sebastian composed his face for the coming conversation. It wouldn't do to sneer at a guest—no matter how odious.

"Dankworth," said Sebastian.

"Your Grace," the man returned. "Do you recall our last conversation?" he asked, sidling closer in his particular greasy manner.

"I do."

"And might you be of assistance to me with a certain, ahem, *lady?*"

The man lifted a suggestive eyebrow, and Sebastian's sneer was provoked into being.

Dankworth had been seeking to become the patron of an opera singer—one with whom Sebastian had had a dalliance with a few years ago. When they'd mutually ended their arrangement, she'd gone on to become the toast of London and then on to Paris. Now, Dankworth wanted "his turn" with her—as if she were an object to be passed around. As if it were his right as a lord and man. The fact was she didn't need Dankworth's patronage— and Sebastian could only suppose she wouldn't want the man as a lover, either.

Here was the seedy underbelly of arts patronage. Sebastian had always been vigilant to stay on the correct side of an admittedly blurry line, but many powerful men entered the arts world with the sole intent of procuring sexual favors.

The imbalance of power turned Sebastian's stomach, and the full brunt of his increasingly foul mood focused on Dankworth. "Who do you take me for, Dankworth?" he asked, low, the question deceptively simple.

"The Duke of Ravensworth, of course," he said on a laugh

that wasn't quite jolly. The gathering of his eyebrows suggested he sensed something amiss.

Sebastian nodded slowly. "Ah, for a moment there, it seemed you were taking me for a procurer of doxies for you."

Dankworth's mouth opened, then snapped shut, a crimson flush crawling up his neck and across his face. That was Dankworth silenced—and everyone within a ten-foot radius who had been gathering in to grab a word edgewise with the Duke of Ravensworth.

Sebastian wasn't finished. "And to be clear, singers and actresses, painters and poets aren't prostitutes. They are artists—many of them at an economic disadvantage. And grubby, grasping men like you know it, don't you?" The circumference around Sebastian and Dankworth expanded, even as ears strained toward the conversation. "So, you use your money and influence as bait to lure them into your bed. You have no care for them as people or artists, only as flesh to be consumed for your own pleasure—and discarded as rubbish once you've had your fill."

Dankworth cleared his throat and averted his gaze, clearly willing himself to be as far away from the Duke of Ravensworth as quickly as possible. The man muttered something unintelligible before scuttling away. Sebastian felt slightly winded from the vehemence of his short speech—and surprised at himself, too. He'd said aloud what he usually kept inside, and for good reason. His efforts to raise funds for the arts weren't likely to attract much coin if he did.

But...perhaps it wasn't only coin that mattered to the arts. Hadn't his time with Ye Olde Albion Players taught him that much? The company lived on words and ideas and mutton-and-potato pasties and their art flourished. Perhaps the arts weren't best served by a top-down endeavor. Perhaps the time had arrived for him to enter a new phase of his support.

Perhaps the time had arrived for him to stop acting like such a bloody duke about it.

Wimberley Hill.

There was his way forward with the arts. It wasn't simply about constructing buildings for the glorification of art; it was also about creating environments where art could grow at its own pace, flourish, and enter the world in its own time.

A sudden frisson of energy sparked through the air, and all eyes flew toward the upper landing of the staircase. Sebastian knew before he looked that the Windermeres had arrived, for the crowd's roar had dulled to a whispery murmur for five solid beats of time. No other arrival could elicit such a response.

Arrayed as a united front in the meager splendor that silk and diamonds could afford their stunning looks, the Windermeres radiated raw glamour, which, in turn, only begot the *ton's* rapt fascination. They were that arresting.

But one was missing.

No Delilah.

Disappointment washed through Sebastian. At ten in the evening, her siblings were already arriving at the farthest edge of fashionably late, though no one would think anything of it. They were the Windermeres. They held and exuded the special something that lit sparks in any room they entered.

Yet the one who sparkled the brightest wasn't with them.

Sebastian might have to accept that summer was well and truly over.

That Delilah would never come to him.

That he hadn't done enough to woo and win her.

Archie took the short flight of steps in two and clapped Sebastian on the back in greeting. "Why the long face, my friend?"

Sebastian willed his usual sardonic smile onto his mouth. That was how to handle Archie. "I'm fairly certain it's its usual length."

Archie laughed and gave him another slap on the back, and the night stretched endless before Sebastian. He didn't have it in him to make jolly with Archie, exchange witticisms with Juliet—who was regarding him even more closely than usual—or even stand beside Ripon and growl his way through the long hours.

Rory stepped forward. "Come on, let's see if anything of interest is happening in the card room." He was regarding Sebastian in a particular way. Rory was like that—deceptively perceptive.

Sebastian shrugged in assent. As the men separated from the ladies, he couldn't help asking. "Won't your wife want to dance or some such?"

"Oh, you know Juliet," said Rory. "She'd much prefer to stand against a wall and watch the goings-on. It's best to leave her to it."

Inside the card room, Sebastian settled at the first table they came to. *Macao*. Probably not the ideal card game to involve himself with, as he was in no mood for bluffing. He placed his markers on crimson felt and was dealt in.

Round after round, he lost, annoying Archie no end, who leaned over and murmured, "You know you're allowed to cheat to win at this one, old chap."

Sebastian cared not.

A server asked if he would like a brandy. He refused. Spirits and a foul mood made for poor bedfellows.

After only a few more rounds of cards, the server reappeared, silver tray extended. Sebastian was again about to refuse it when a spray of blue caught his eye. Upon the tray lay not a tumbler of brandy, but a flower. A cornflower...

A *wildflower*.

His head whipped around, and he gave the room a quick scan, half rising to gain a clear view.

No sign of her.

He let his cards fall onto the felt, where they landed face up. A collective groan sounded around the table. He'd ruined the hand. What did he care?

He'd just received a wildflower.

A tentative, fragile feeling took wing inside him.

"All well with you?" asked Rory, clearly annoyed. Even his patience had its limits.

"I, erm," said Sebastian, "require the bog."

All eyebrows to a one lifted toward the ceiling.

Well, not Ripon's. He snorted.

"The *bog?*" asked Archie.

Generally speaking, dukes didn't refer to the necessary room as the bog.

Sebastian supposed summer wasn't over quite yet—in more ways than one. In for a penny, in for a pound... He shot to his feet. "Immediately," he tossed over his shoulder, his feet already on the move.

He caught up with the server and snatched the cornflower off the tray. "Who gave this to you?" he asked, trying not to sound too commanding. After all, this man was in his employ.

"A scullery, Your Grace."

Sebastian stepped outside the room and glanced both ways down the corridor. Though scattered with several lords and ladies—some passing through, others paired off for private conversation—Sebastian immediately saw Delilah wasn't one of them. But he did spot something on the marble floor ten or so feet away.

A yellow tansy.

Another wildflower.

He picked it up and followed its direction, the crowd decreasing in density as the trail of flowers led him away from the ballroom. It occurred to him after he'd collected his fifth flower that he was acquiring a bouquet, with a few guests casting befuddled second glances his way. What was the Duke of Ravensworth doing holding a wildflower nosegay? Others even tried to catch his attention. He ignored them all.

Dead rude of him, of course. He gave a mental shrug. He was Ravensworth.

Except...to the woman at the end of this wildflower path, he was Seb, too.

Or that was what the feeling surging inside him hoped.

He followed the path into his study and turned the lock behind him. Delilah must've done a bit of talking to wheedle her way into his private domain. The scullery, he suspected. Delilah wasn't the sort to use her feminine wiles on men to get what she wanted. Rather, she would've turned to the girl no one hardly noticed and given her attention.

She would be a good duchess.

His step faltered. *Careful*, a small voice warned. It wouldn't do to get ahead of himself.

The path continued outside to the stone terrace and down a short staircase into his private garden. Every house he owned had a private terrace and garden. Many privileges were afforded a duke, but so too were many demands placed on him. A private domain that only he inhabited was necessary.

It would be Delilah who infiltrated it.

And of course, the wildflower path led to the folly, a ten-year-old structure constructed to look like a Grecian temple on the verge of falling down. Of course, it wasn't. It was quite structurally sound, in fact.

He took the steps two at a time and came to a sudden stop at the threshold. Lit by a single ray of the waxing moon in the center of the space stood his folly. *Delilah*. A vision in gold: gold silk dress, gold bandeau in her gold hair, gold silk mask. *A goddess.*

Suddenly awkward as a green youth of sixteen years, he held out his handful of wildflowers. "These are yours, I believe."

She reached out and accepted them. A seriousness in clear blue eyes that usually twinkled with mischief, she canted her head slightly. "I always wanted to attend a masquerade ball."

"I know."

Chapter Fifteen

T HE BREATH CAUGHT in Delilah's chest.
She could almost laugh at herself.
Here she was acting like a heroine in a romance.
Again.
But there was no help for it.
Dressed in his evening blacks, with his dashing silk domino, Sebastian was devastating.
And this devastating man had thrown a masquerade ball simply for her.
The opening notes of a waltz drifted along on air gone light with possibility. Drawn in by the music—by their own need to be closer to one another—they each took a step forward, then another, until her silk-gloved hand was sliding into his large, strong one, his other hand finding the indent of her waist, his warmth slipping through layers of silk and muslin and into her. Wordlessly, their feet began to move to the music, but slowly, half a beat to every one of the string quartet. Here, in this folly, they weren't bound by rules or other people's ideas of who they were or should be.
Only what they wanted mattered.
Only who they were to each other.
Words would matter—eventually—but not in this moment as

he pulled her closer, her body stretched against the full length of his. Where she was soft, he was hard. The strength latent in that long, muscular body of his amazed her anew each time she felt it.

But really, why should it? Sebastian was strong in every way. It wasn't simply his physical person. He was strong in his loyalties and in his passions, inspiring a responding loyalty and passion within her. How seductive his combination of strengths.

She lifted onto the tips of her toes, and her mouth met his ear. Her tongue followed.

A groan rumbled through his chest. "Delilah," he murmured.

It was true he was a strong man.

But she knew where his weakness lay.

A weakness she fully intended to exploit.

His hand tightened on her waist, pulling her closer, an action at odds with his mutter of protest. Well, she wasn't about to make this easy on him. She trailed lower, down his neck, his hard, steady pulse beneath her mouth. Then she sucked the sensitive skin, and his breath took on a ragged quality.

Ah...there.

His resistance was slipping.

Still, she sensed a tension in him.

His resistance wasn't entirely vanquished.

"We need to talk, Delilah."

"We do," she agreed before giving the space behind his ear another lick. He liked it there. Then she pulled back to meet his gaze. "In my defense, I did fully intend to talk first tonight."

"This won't solve anything," he protested. His golden gaze held an unmovable quality.

Dukes.

Yet his hand slid around to the small of her back. Her hips crushed into his, and the hard length of his fully erect manhood made the breath stick in her lungs. Oh, the feel of him...

She needed it.

Now.

"Here's the thing, Sebastian," she said. "I can't arrive at any reasonable thought until we have *this* out of the way."

"*This?*" Humor flashed behind his eyes. She sensed an opening.

"Do you have any idea how devastating you are?" she asked. Now, it was her voice fraying at the edges.

Arrogance now radiated off him in waves. "I've been told."

Oh, how ridiculously attractive was his arrogance.

It should annoy—possibly infuriate—her.

Instead, it made her want to rip every last shred of clothing off his body.

Toward that end, she reached up and took his white silk cravat in hand.

She rather liked having this duke by the throat.

His feet slowed to a stop. "Delilah."

"Mmm?" she mumbled, distracted. "This knot is the work of the devil."

"It's actually the work of my valet." Sebastian still held that unmovable quality in his eye. He jutted his chin toward the manse. "There is a bed not fifty feet from here."

Her fingers kept busy, finally making some headway. "We've never needed one before." It was only the truth.

His hands covered hers, stilling them. "Come," he said, twining her fingers through his.

They did make it up the stone staircase to his study, but only as far as the door before Delilah seized an opportunity and pulled his head down for a kiss. Instinctively, he returned it, pressing her against the doorjamb, his body fully against hers. Her leg had no choice but to wrap around his waist, leaving her sex no option but to grind against his length. Oh, the hard, delicious feel of him…

"This is close enough to a bed," she muttered against his mouth.

Her wants were simple.

All she wanted was him.

Here.

145

Now.

But he was in no mood to oblige her.

On a tormented groan—oh, why did the man insist on torturing both of them—he wrenched away, reaching for her hand again, leading her inside his private study, through a secret door in a bookcase—she would be asking about that later...*after*—and up a dark, narrow staircase. Halfway up the stairs, she reached up and squeezed his taut arse. Of its own accord, her hand snaked around and dragged across his hot, swollen manhood.

His step faltered. "Delilah," came a warning without much conviction behind it.

She sensed she could have him here.

But he wanted her in a bed.

And she supposed she was learning relationships were about compromise.

Then they were stepping inside his bedroom. The only lighting was a low fire in the hearth and a few dim sconces on the walls. But there was enough light for her to see this was very much a duke's bedroom—all done in deep blue silks and velvets, impeccably tasteful and immaculate. She would expect nothing less from Sebastian.

He turned and caught her about the waist. "At last, we made it to a bedroom."

She laughed. She couldn't help it.

Then she met his eyes, and the dark intention within, and her smile slipped as he shrugged off coat and waistcoat. He closed the distance between them, then his hands were making short work of the buttons on the side of her dress. It hadn't yet reached the floor before he was turning her around, loosening the knots of her stays, the garment slipping off her body to join her dress. She took the silk tips of her gloves between her teeth and tugged them off, leaving her clad in naught but chemise, stockings, and slippers. Then the chemise was over her head and joining the other garments on the deep-piled Aubusson carpet.

"The mask can stay," said Sebastian. His serious, golden eyes slowly raked over her, growing black in the flickering firelight. "There's something I want you to do." He hesitated. "And you can say no."

She reached up and clasped her hands around his neck, stretching her naked body against his fully clothed one, a smile curling her mouth. No doubt it was a wicked one. "There is nothing you could ask of me that I would say no to." Her tongue swiped across her bottom lip. His gaze followed the motion. "So, ask."

"I want you"—he took a step forward, coaxing a step back from her...a step for nearly every word he spoke—"to lay on my bed"—his mouth met her ear—"and spread your legs...*wide*."

A feeling, dark and sinuous, snaked through Delilah. What he was asking of her would push her limits.

And she understood something she hadn't known before.

She wanted those limits pushed.

"Then I want you to touch yourself."

The backs of her knees bumped against the bed. Her gaze held his. "While you watch?" she asked through the frisson of mild shock that traced through her.

What a thing to want, and yet...

Didn't she like to be watched?

"Yes."

Oh, the flame of lust that licked through her as she released her hands from around his neck and perched onto the foot of the bed. He grabbed a chair and sank into it, his gaze hot upon her as she spread her legs...*wide*.

Her quim open and exposed like this... She'd had no idea this was what went on between men and women in bedrooms.

One hand planted behind her for support, the other trailed down her body, slowly, teasingly. She took a nipple between forefinger and thumb and pinched. His chest utterly still, no breath entered or left his lungs, and she understood the full extent of her power.

She had the devastating, arrogant Duke of Ravensworth in

the palm of her hand. "You like that?" she couldn't help asking.

She couldn't help the note of triumph in her voice, either.

"Oh, yes," he rumbled.

"You want more?"

A smile tipped at one corner of his mouth. He understood a game was underway. "What do you have in mind?"

"Remove that devilish cravat."

Hers was the power make demands.

Efficient fingers reached up and made quick work of the offending garment, and he flung it away, his shirt flopping open.

Her hand trailed lower, down the soft skin of her stomach to the even softer mound of her mons pubis, stopping there. "Shirt," she said. "*Off.*"

Fine muslin lifted over and off his head, joining the cravat on the floor. Now it was her gaze rapt upon him. Well, his bare torso—and the defined muscles rippling beneath skin fuzzed with golden hair.

Of their own accord, her fingers slid lower, meeting the slickness of her sex, grazing the sensitive nub that throbbed...*ached*...with the desire to be touched...

By the man before her.

Her fingers would do.

For now.

Oh, but watching him watch her touch herself...

How very wicked.

"Are you wet?" he asked.

She nodded and gave herself a stroke.

"How wet?"

"Dripping," rasped across her throat.

What a wicked thing to say.

But was the truth ever really wicked?

Sometimes.

"Lower," he said.

She obeyed.

"Enter yourself." he said.

Her gaze caught his and knowingly swept down his body—coming to a stop on the hard, distinct outline of his manhood. "Unbutton your trousers," she countered.

Oh, she wanted to see *him* as she stroked herself. If she couldn't have him inside her, she would ravish him with her eyes as her fingers made for a poor substitute.

Button by button, he freed himself.

Rigid and thick, his cockstand made quite a spectacle of itself.

Tit for tat, her finger slid along her sex, lighting up nerve endings all the way, and as she entered herself, he took his shaft in hand and gave himself a long, deliberate stroke.

She exhaled a groan of pleasure—but one with unsatisfied edges.

She wanted *that* inside her. Watching him touch himself... It pulled something new from her. Each time they'd been together, she'd wanted him with every cell of her being. But the way she wanted him now... It was heightened.

It was as if she would die of want without him.

A feeling began to gather in the center of her, pulling her tight with building need. "Sebastian," she said. Nay, not *said*. Pleaded...*begged*. "I want you inside me when I..." she trailed, unable to finish a thought, much less a sentence.

Without taking his eyes off her, or his hand off himself, he rose and stepped forward, his solid, muscular form making way between her legs, his manhood only inches from where she wanted it—inside her.

Yet, oh, it felt so far away.

He didn't grab her legs like she all but demanded—or plunge inside her like her quim all but demanded. Instead, he tucked his thumb beneath her chin, tipped her head back, and pressed his mouth to hers. Slowly, thoroughly, he kissed her until she was a senseless, trembly bundle of need.

Deliberately, he pressed forward, so she lay flat on her back and he hovered above her, supporting himself with an elbow to the side of her head, his body angled so his manhood slid against her mons pubis. Then he was entering her with a single smooth stroke, filling her to her limit—and beyond it.

"Sebastian," she breathed out as tingly sensation swept through her. "You were correct."

"About?"

"This does feel better in a bed."

His smile against her neck as he plunged deeper inside her, that felt good, too.

Everything with this man felt good...too good.

She hoped he truly meant what he'd started.

Because she was never letting him go.

Chapter Sixteen

THE FEEL OF Delilah…of being inside her…the press of their naked bodies slicked with sweat against each other…her sex tight around him…her hips angled as if she couldn't get enough…

In his bed.

Now that he had her here, he might never let her leave it.

She was so potent a temptation that she brought out the medieval warlord in him.

Claim…possess… That was one way to have her—as bodies designed solely to pleasure one another.

But he wanted her as more than her body.

He wanted all of her—and he wanted it given freely.

This act of mutual pleasure was a giving—not a taking.

So much of their relations with one another felt rooted in the physical. But it was the feeling beneath pleasured nerve endings that gave the act true satisfaction. It wasn't simply a meeting of complimentary body parts. It channeled deeper to a place inside him that had ever remained untouched.

Until this summer.

And as he plunged in and out of her, he poured all that feeling into the act. This wasn't claiming and possessing—well, it was that, too. But it wasn't *only* claiming and possessing. It was also wooing and winning.

Her teeth found one of his nipples and bit lightly. Sparks lit through him, and his mouth found her neck and sucked as he plunged harder, deeper. "Oh, Sebastian," she groaned.

Sharp fingernails were now scraping down his back, demanding more of him—all he had—*deeper...faster.*

Sometimes wooing and winning looked remarkably like claiming and possessing.

Felt like it, too.

Her legs wrapped around him, heels digging into the muscles of his arse. Her eyes closed, her head arched back; she was close, he felt it in the tension of her body. She was on the hunt for release, straining toward its promise as it taunted and tempted her just out of reach.

And seeing her so close brought him close. He wanted to prolong this union of their bodies—never wanted it to end, in fact. A nigh impossible feat with her reaching for climax with him inside her.

Perhaps Delilah had the right of it, and it would be best to get this tup out of the way.

No.

He tempered the rhythm of his hips and began entering her with slow deliberation. Her eyes flew open in outrage. She'd been so close and now he was denying her.

But he wasn't.

This wasn't a denial of pleasure.

This was a prolonging of it.

In and out of her, he moved, every part of themselves mingling—their breath, their sweat, their sexes. A taking of pleasure in the journey, not the end.

That was what beds were good for.

For taking one's time, and doing it right.

The outrage drained from eyes, and in its place he detected surrender to sensation. She had much to learn about this act—this union—its ebbs and flows...the possibility that reached far beyond the shore.

But—too soon for his liking—his body's demands would be put off no longer, and he found himself driving into her with focused intensity. Her body responded instantly, her hips angling to receive more of him. Greedy for it, in fact. "You're a wanton, Lady Delilah."

"Were you ever in doubt?" she asked between moans of pleasure.

Actually..."No."

Some part of him had known these last few years that it would be like this between them. *Greedy...insatiable...unquench-able.*

An appetite ever unsated.

A thirst never quenched.

That was what existed between him and Delilah.

And ever would.

Relentlessly, he drove into her, pushing her to the brink of release. Then she tipped over just when he was certain he could no longer hold off his own climax. Mindlessly, he plunged in and out of her, shouting his release to the rafters beyond the coffered ceiling. They likely heard it in the ballroom.

He cared not.

He was Ravensworth.

And the woman beneath him presently floating outside her body in the exquisite ether of satiety was his future duchess.

His eyes drifted closed for a moment...

A faraway clock chimed one, and Sebastian's eyes flew open in a sudden panic only assuaged when he registered Delilah's body beside him. Her mask was gone.

"You drifted off," she said, a little smile fluttering about her lips.

Lips that looked very much like they wanted to be kissed. He knew that look in her eyes.

And so did his cock, which was already at half-mast.

No.

Not yet.

He rolled away from her and off the bed, then unhurriedly crossed the room and grabbed his trousers. His half-mast cock must be put away for the talk he and Delilah needed to have.

She sat up and pulled the sheet over her breasts. He supposed it was necessary that they, too, be hidden from view.

He took a seat in the chair he'd vacated not an hour ago, sitting back lazily, legs sprawled. When he'd last sat here, he'd been exclusively focused on the carnal. Now, he had a different intent. "The door's there," he said, pointing across the room, as if making idle chit-chat. He pointed the other direction. "And another one over there."

Sebastian hadn't realized until this very moment an anger toward Delilah had been simmering inside him.

Knowledge shone in her clear azure eyes. She knew—and understood.

Still, he couldn't seem to let it go. "In case you want to run, of course."

And there it was as concrete as a boulder in the space between them. The source of his anger...

She'd run.

And not toward him.

"I'm not going anywhere, Sebastian."

A measure of tension released from his body. But it wasn't enough. How he wanted to believe her—but he wasn't yet sure he could. "Are you certain?"

They both understood the question held multiple layers. It wasn't simply about staying in his bed for one night. It was about staying in his life...forever.

Was she sure?

She gathered the sheet about herself and moved to the foot of the bed, her blond curls tossed wildly about her head. She looked deliciously sleep- and love-tousled, and it was all he could do to remain still.

But this wouldn't work between them if he followed his body's urging and made love to her now.

She must come to him.

The other could come later...*if*...

"It occurs to me that you likely think I run because I fear consequences."

"The thought has occurred to me."

"In truth, I never minded a spot of trouble." A dry laugh escaped her. "A Windermere trait, to be sure."

Sebastian remained silent while she worked her way up to saying what was on her mind.

"This is difficult to explain, but when I feel something, I feel it exceedingly deeply. *Passionately*. Too passionately, really," she said on a self-deprecating laugh.

He wished she wouldn't do that, but he kept his silence.

"And when something that I want goes all to hell, I have great difficulty bearing it. It's as if the disappointment crashes down onto me like an avalanche and utterly overwhelms me." She exhaled a shaky breath. "So, I run and find something else to occupy me for a time, until the feeling passes, which has been known to take weeks, even months."

"You ignore your feelings?"

Delilah nodded. "I do quite a bang-up job of it, in fact. No one wants to see a mopey Windermere."

And like that, Sebastian's anger drained away. "You can't ignore your feelings forever."

"So I've learned." She bit her bottom lip between straight white teeth. "The night of my lead performance, I ran again."

"I noticed."

"But not because Oliver Quincy exposed me and denied me what I wanted. That was my excuse."

"Pardon?"

"To play the lead role on that stage wasn't what I'd come to truly want."

"Delilah, it was everything you ever wanted."

She shook her head. "No longer. What I truly wanted was *you*."

"*Me?*" The next instant he was giving voice to a cynical thought. "That's been well established." He jutted his chin. "In that very bed tonight, in fact."

He refused to consider another meaning.

Not unless she spoke it.

"*You*, Sebastian. Not your body—well, that too—but *you*. I'd come to want you with such a passion that it overwhelmed me. So, I ran."

"You were running from me?" he asked, just to be clear she was saying what he thought she was saying.

She nodded.

"How is that better?" He failed to see it.

Her face became utterly transformed with fervor. "Because I had to run from you to discover that you were my destination all along."

Her words—the raw sincerity of her voice—provoked a feeling inside him. A feeling that wanted to take wing. After all, she'd just spoken the very words he'd been wanting to hear. But... "Delilah, be careful with your words. Once you consent to be mine, you're mine forever. There's no more running."

She appeared to be weighing his words. "I'll always need to feel free. The mistress and orchestrator of my own fate."

"I know." And he respected and admired that about her.

"But I've learned I need something else equally as much."

"Which is?"

"A partner...*you*," she said simply. "What's the point if you're not by my side? It would only be a life half lived."

She slid off the foot of the bed, her bare feet padding silently across the carpet, step by deliberate step, sheet held to her throat, dragging on the floor behind her. Sebastian's heart raced in his chest, anticipation rioting through him. The tender look in her eyes spoke greater volumes than words ever could.

In a way, this was her running again...

Toward him...

Her destination.

She straddled his legs and lowered to a perch on his thighs, her light scent of rose and Delilah swirling through the air. Nothing separated them now.

"Every part of me is yours, Sebastian." Her gaze shone clear and direct and honest. "I'm your wildflower."

"Does that make me your sun?"

She gave his arm a light swat. "Arrogant man."

A novel thought struck him. "And you love that about me."

A seriousness entered her eyes. "No."

Sebastian's stomach plummeted to his feet.

"I don't simply love that about you. I love *you*."

He reached out and took her face in his hands, her cheeks soft beneath his rough palms. "And I love you, my wildflower."

She nuzzled into his touch, then said, "About the document you sent me."

He'd been wondering when that subject would be broached. He'd also been wondering if he would hold to its implicit demand—that she marry him—in the face of her opposition. He suspected it wouldn't take much for her to convince him to live in sin with her forever. Still... "Before you say no—"

"Who says my answer is *no*?"

"Is it *yes*?"

"Not yet."

"I shall not force you."

"You couldn't if you tried."

"Not even if I promised you that we could do what we just did in that bed every day for the rest of our lives?"

"Perhaps then."

"Well, I'm not promising you that."

"Then the answer is definitely *no*."

"Delilah..."

"We can be Sebastian and Delilah. And Seb and Lilah. And..." She slid off her perch on his legs and sank to her knees beside the chair and took his hands in hers, her head tipped back so she could hold his gaze "And we can be duke and duchess, if you'll have me."

It took a moment for Sebastian to grasp the meaning behind her words. "Are you proposing marriage to me, Delilah?"

Eyes suddenly bright with a sheen of unshed tears, she stared up at him, imploring, and nodded. Her passion was there for him to see. She wanted him—a life with him—with all her being—and it scared her. But she didn't run. She'd planted her feet and remained. Her passion was a gift.

"In three days, at two o'clock in the afternoon, at St. Paul's Cathedral," she began, each phrase emerging staccato, "I'll be standing at the head of the aisle with the archbishop—"

"The archbishop?"

"He's a close friend of Amelia's mother-in-law," she said, impatient, as if it were beside the point. "Will you join me there? And pledge your troth to me forever?"

Sebastian joined her on the floor. She reached her arms around his neck, and he gathered her close, their mouths only inches apart. "I shall."

The serious look in her eyes told him she had something more to say. "But be careful, Sebastian," she muttered against his lips.

"Why is that?" he rumbled.

"Because once I make you mine, there will be no end of earth that you could run that I wouldn't pursue you."

And as Sebastian pulled his future duchess tight against him, in the moment just before he pressed his mouth to hers, he said, "I can't think of a fate I would rather suffer."

Epilogue

Wimberley Hill
Spring 1824

WHAT A TERRIBLE *waste.*

That was the first thought that crossed Oliver Quincy's mind as he alighted from his hired carriage and glanced about the palatial country estate of the Duke of Ravensworth.

Why in the name of all that was right and proper had His Grace turned this grand monument to his and England's glory over to a parcel of artists of unknown parentage?

But then, the Duke had improvidently married a Windermere, so the curious workings of the Duke's mind would ever remain opaque to him.

Quincy quite conveniently put it from his mind that he himself had, in fact, proposed marriage to Lady Delilah Windermere—more than once.

A young laughing fellow dressed as a donkey pressed a leaflet into his hand. Emblazoned in bold lettering was *Warrior of Earth and Skye* by The Right Honorable Viscountess Kilmuir. He squinted and kept reading only to find the music had been composed by Lord and Lady Archer, both of whom would be performing it, as well. The set design and painted backdrops had been created by the Duke and Duchess of Ripon. And in the lead role of the maiden warrior Scáthach would be none other than the Duchess of Ravensworth.

A mild frisson of shock traced through Quincy. He'd hoped now that the Windermeres were illustriously married and titled, they would've settled a bit. But it was clear for all to see the Windermeres were still very much the Windermeres. Shocking, indeed, but not altogether surprising.

Along with scores of other guests possessed of the low look of local villagers—not a single silk dress or proper accent amongst the lot—Quincy followed the indicated granite path, all manner of colorful bunting and streamers flapping riotously about. This was precisely why one didn't leave the running of a grand estate to artists. All dignity and sense of station flew out the window.

He sniffed and pulled himself up to his fullest height. Still, it was a duke's estate, and Quincy's invited presence here said something about his rising status in Society—local villagers in attendance notwithstanding. One must placate the locals. As a duke, Ravensworth would understand as much.

The granite path ended, and Quincy stepped onto the top landing of the amphitheater that everyone was talking about. A summons to view a performance at Wimberley Hill was one of the most highly sought-after invitations in the *ton*.

Of course, he'd received one.

His gaze cast about, on the prowl for other Society luminaries such as himself. A few rows down, mingled amongst the commoners—truly, there might be more commoners than nobles—he struck gold. There stood a statuesque lord and lady of middling-to-late years whose graying hair picked up the pinks and purples of the sunset in the distance. Or...were they wearing dyed wigs? One wouldn't put such a thing past the Earl and Countess of Cumberland if the fancy took them. After all, their progeny had inherited their wild, scandalous ways from someone.

Seeing no one else in the crowd he recognized, Quincy sidled closer to the Earl and Countess, crossed his arms over his chest, and nodded at every conversational pause as if he had the slightest understanding of what they were on about. Something about theater structures.

Truly, these Windermeres.

)⫞⫰

LORD FRANCIS WINDERMERE, the Earl of Cumberland, watched his countess Augusta give the unfamiliar young-ish gentleman who had quite unaccountably joined them a cursory once-over before continuing. "I'm simply saying that I'm not sure we can call this theater a true amphitheater. It does have the sloping seating and is built into the side of a hill, but it doesn't fully encircle the stage, like the one at Pompeii."

"Ah, Pompeii," said the strange gentleman on a knowing nod. The man appeared quite settled in.

"I would posit," continued Augusta, "that this stage is actually more similar to an English one from the era of Queen Elizabeth."

"A mongrel stage, if you will," said Francis with a mischievous smile. He ever flashed his wife that smile when she rode on her purist high horse.

She swatted his arm playfully. "Oh, Francis, you're having me on."

"A bit," he conceded. Someone had to guide his countess into the forest when she was lost amongst the trees.

A high-pitched laugh sounded at their side. As one, Francis and Augusta shifted their attention toward the gentleman who seemed to have barnacled himself onto them. "And who might you be?" she asked, ever direct with a point. Francis loved that about his countess.

Self-satisfied, the gentleman rocked from heel to toe. "You'll know me as Mr. Oliver Quincy, of course."

A confused beat of time ticked past. "Who?" asked Augusta.

Again, Mr. Quincy laughed. "No one will doubt where Lord Archer gets his sense of humor."

Vague recollection came to Francis. "You're the fellow who proposed marriage to Delilah."

Augusta's brow crinkled. "Two…or was it three times?"

"Ah, the japes of youth," said Mr. Quincy, utterly unabashed.

Undecided as to how to manage this curious social interaction—truly, it was a first—Francis offered Mr. Quincy a shallow bow, which the gentleman accepted as his due with a gracious nod of the head. "Now if you will excuse us," began Francis, "we must—"

He'd never been any good at delivering an untruth. It was a fine thing he ever had his countess with him. "We must go stand over there," she said, pointing toward a patch of ground twenty feet away.

Well, she wasn't much more skilled at it.

However, the excuse did land them in a spot of good luck, for *over there* stood Delilah and the unlikely man who had become her husband—the Duke of Ravensworth.

Delilah, a duchess...

Amelia as a duchess aligned with what he only expected of his eldest daughter, but Delilah...

Francis gave his head the subtle shake he always did at the unlikely outcome.

⚓

FROM THE CORNER of his eye, Sebastian noticed Delilah's parents approaching. But it was Delilah who needed him at this moment. She was a bit of a thoroughbred, his wife—always requiring some shushing and soothing before a performance. "All is under control," he said. "Would I have it any other way?"

For the dozenth time in as many minutes, she dug her watch from her dress pocket, which was no simple negotiation given that she was presently eight months gone with child. He only just refrained from rubbing his hand across the tight drum of her belly. It wouldn't be appreciated in this moment. But really, their first child was nearly here. Familiar twin feelings of joy and anxiety streaked through him.

Having checked the time, Delilah settled. "You're correct, of course."

"Now, Ravensworth," said his mother-in-law by way of greeting. "What would you say was the primary influence for this amphitheater? More Roman? Or Elizabethan?"

Sebastian smiled. The Countess wasn't one to be fobbed off with a shallow answer. That in mind, he said, "You'll have to ask the architect, who is two rows down." He pointed toward said gentleman. "Would you like an introduction?"

⫶⋞

DELILAH SAW HER opportunity to duck out and seized it. Her parents could keep a conversation about ancient structures going until the wee hours of the morning—and she had other fish to fry. Like the fact that she was to take to the stage in fewer than fifteen minutes.

She made her way along the periphery of the seating, and her nerves began to fall away when she joined the other actors and crew. It was an atmosphere that ever enlivened her—even at eight months along with child. If she were being dead honest, she might prefer to be lounging on a cushy settee, feet propped atop an ottoman. But then she would miss *this*—the energy and chaos in the moments leading up to a performance.

And she wouldn't miss it for anything.

One happy coincidence about her swollen belly was that it provided a convenient shelf for reading material. She utilized it now as she ran through lines with the talented young actress who would be playing her daughter, Uathach.

"Has anyone in the history of pregnant women ever been as pregnant as I?" she asked, not expecting anyone to answer.

"Me," came a voice behind her.

She turned and found Juliet approaching, one arm linked with Valentina, who said, "And me."

It was true. Juliet and Valentina's bellies might have rivaled even hers. They were, indeed, three of the most pregnant women to ever walk the face of the earth.

Amelia, ever her busy self, approached, paintbrush in hand which she'd been using to touch up the backdrops. "Well, Amelia," said Delilah, "at least for once you find yourself without child."

A smile twitched about one corner of Amelia's mouth. The particular secret smile she'd developed since meeting Ripon.

"Amelia..." began Delilah, a feeling about the root of her sister's secret smile quickly gaining momentum.

"I wouldn't go so far as to say I'm without child," she said, rubbing her palm across her subtly rounded stomach.

"No!" gasped Delilah.

Amelia's smile broadened, not so secret anymore. "Oh, yes."

Juliet laughed, and Valentina reached out and squeezed Amelia's hand in congratulation.

"Your third child in four years, Amelia," said Delilah. "Are you trying to set a breeding record? You always were competitive."

"I happen to enjoy babies," said Amelia, simply, and no one could refute the honesty.

"How many children do you plan on having?" asked Valentina.

Amelia opened her mouth to answer, but it was Ripon who stepped forward and answered. "When we have enough to field a cricket team."

"Eleven?" asked Juliet with the lift of a dubious eyebrow.

"Perhaps we could include cousins, Tristan," said Amelia, who herself looked doubtful about the prospect of eight more pregnancies in her future.

"I'll consider it."

Amelia playfully swatted her husband's arm. She didn't used to be the sort of woman who playfully swatted men on the arm. And really, she still wasn't—only Ripon could provoke her into such coquettish behavior.

"I believe your skills are still required on the backdrop, my sweet," he continued.

)ど

As Ripon and Amelia stepped to their task, Archie slid into their place, taking his wife's hand and delivering a quick kiss to the elegant curve of her neck. Valentina understood Society's expectation that she would chastise her husband for such overt and mildly carnal displays of affection. But why should she when she loved every ounce of his ardor and exuberance—even when it strayed into scandalous territory?

"Time for the music to commence, my love," he murmured into her ear.

)ど

Archie and Valentina had been gone not three seconds when Rory arrived, holding a...

Juliet's brow crinkled. "Is that a wind chime, husband?"

Rory waved his arm so the tubes would knock against each other. "You know, for ambience."

Juliet flashed her cousin a knowing smirk. "Delilah, is this your none-too-subtle way of keeping Rory and me as far from the stage as possible?"

"If you wouldn't mind," said Delilah. "Your writing skills are unparalleled, my lovely Juliet, but leave the acting to the professionals."

"I believe the actress who plays Uathach is requesting a few changes to her lines," Rory cut in.

"No changing the lines," said Delilah. She possessed more than a smidge of her mother's purist outlook.

Juliet couldn't help laughing. "Oh, Delilah, words and language are ever evolving, and I'm no Shakespeare."

"True, you're not," said Rory, utterly serious. "You're Lady

Juliet Macbeth."

A frisson of warmth stole through Juliet. Her husband often incited that feeling inside her.

Still, she wanted to hear what the actress had to say, so she took her protective husband's large, masculine hand in hers, and led him—and his wind chime—away.

SEBASTIAN TOOK HIS place beside Delilah, so they stood quiet in their space of two within the frenetic hustle and bustle of backstage before a performance. She felt a kick in her belly and placed his hand on the spot. Together, they waited for another kick in stillness and silence. Then it came, and they both smiled. "She will be like her mother, methinks," he said.

"You cannot know we're having a girl." Delilah hoped her secret wish for her first child to be female didn't show on her face—but she suspected it did. "I could be carrying your future heir."

He shook his head. "You'll have a girl first, my duchess."

"Regardless," she said, consulting her pocket watch yet again, "I'm fairly certain the ghost of Scáthach will haunt me for the remainder of my days for portraying her while heavily with child."

"Scáthach had a daughter and was the mightiest warrior in Scotland." Sebastian's hand found the small of Delilah's back and pulled her close. He jutted his chin toward the stage, which sat ready and waiting for the performance. "You'll have the audience—and the ghost of Scáthach—sitting in the palm of your hand out there."

Delilah stared up at this improbable husband of hers and experienced such a strong surge of tenderness that the breath caught in her chest. "All *this*"—she swept her arm around—"none of it is possible without you."

A demurring smile curved his mouth, and he gave his head a

small shake. "Delilah—"

He would make light of what she was about to say.

And she wasn't about to let him.

"It's your vision, skill, and determination that saw Wimberley Hill go from dream to reality. These actors, painters, writers, musicians… They all have *you* to thank. And *I*, Sebastian," she continued through the emotion clogging her throat, "I have you to thank for this life. *Our* life."

She found that she had much to say to this husband of hers, and she couldn't stop now, though she sensed everyone waiting for her. What she needed to say here, to him, was of much more vital importance than anything she would say on that stage tonight.

Oh, what a changed woman she was that that could be true.

"Without you, I would've lived a life of frustration. You freed me." Delilah rubbed her rounded belly. "And this babe—be it boy or girl—will be the most fortunate child in the world to call you father."

"I'd like her to call me Papa."

Delilah wouldn't be deterred by levity. Archie was her brother, after all, so she was well accustomed to such attempts—and how to sidestep them. "And *I* am the most fortunate wife in the world to call you husband." Tears broke free and slipped down her cheeks. "I love our life, Seb. I love *you*."

THIS TENDER AND vulnerable Delilah in his arms, Sebastian couldn't have predicted her a few years ago. When he'd first fallen for her, he'd been drawn by the brilliance of her light, but he hadn't suspected that another light lay behind it. A softer light. A light warm and nurturing. A light that invited growth and bloom. He cupped the back of her head and angled his own down for a kiss—a kiss that ever sparked kindling inside him.

Later, after the play was performed and the audience was on

its feet in rapturous applause, Delilah rushed backstage as fast as her belly would allow and found Sebastian in the wings. She took his hand and said, "You're coming with me."

If Sebastian had known she was going to pull him onto the boards, he might've offered some resistance. But now he stood in a line with all the Windermeres and their respective spouses, and he was glad as he scanned the crowd beyond the stage lights and found the figure he sought. A smile curved his mouth.

Oliver Quincy.

Delilah had been utterly confounded when he'd insisted on inviting the man. "But he's an absolute twit."

"True."

"And he ruined my one night in a featured role with the Albion Players," she said, the grudge she yet harbored understandably deep.

"Also true."

Nothing his wife said ran counter to Sebastian's feelings regarding Quincy, but he'd held firm in his determination to extend the man an invitation. For one simple reason: Sebastian would be forever indebted to Oliver Quincy.

He'd made Delilah run…

To him.

What Sebastian knew was that Oliver Quincy—absolute twit that he was—would always find good favor with the Duke of Ravensworth. He squeezed his wife's hand and let her warmth— her *fire*—blaze through him as he met Quincy's eye and nodded.

OLIVER QUINCY RETURNED the Duke of Ravensworth's nod, as he stood with the rest of the audience. Truly, he could hardly countenance his good fortune.

It was a moment of honesty and self-reflection that passed quickly.

Why wouldn't a duke defer to him, really? And send him

invitations to exclusive performances that had the rest of the *ton* gagging with envy?

No matter that this particular event—really, a duchess heavy with child waddling about a stage wielding a battle axe!—held not the slightest bit of interest for him. But it did confirm the man of quality he was. Others would have to take notice.

And yet...

He couldn't help but squint against their reflected glory. Gads, those Windermeres were tall and striking...*excessively* tall and striking. Their height and good looks and general charm bordered on the garish.

It was simply that those Windermeres appeared so very and unapologetically...

In love.

More than a trifle gauche to be so very, unapologetically—*excessively*—in love.

But also, it had to be admitted, so very, unapologetically—*excessively*—Windermere.

The End

About the Author

Sofie Darling is an award-winning author of historical romance. The third book in her Shadows and Silk series, Her Midnight Sin, won the 2020 RONE award for Best Historical Regency.

She spent much of her twenties raising two boys and reading every romance she could get her hands on. Once she realized she simply had to write the books she loved, she finished her English degree and embarked on her writing career. Mr. Darling and the boys gave her their wholehearted blessing.

When she's not writing heroes who make her swoon, she runs a marathon in a different state every year, visits crumbling medieval castles whenever she gets a chance, and enjoys a slightly codependent relationship with her beagle, Bosco.

Lightning Source UK Ltd.
Milton Keynes UK
UKHW021933030223
416465UK00023B/264